THE THIRTEEN TRULY GREAT THINGS OF LIFE

BY

HAROLD BELL WRIGHT

To Mrs. Elsbery W. Reynolds

In admiration of the splendid motherhood that, in her sons, has contributed such wealth of manhood to the race. And, in her daughter, has given to human-kind such riches of womanhood. With kindest regards, I inscribe this book.

H. B. W.

"Relay Heights" June 8, 1912

Behold the child, by Nature's kindly law, Pleased with a rattle, tickled with a straw; Some livelier plaything gives his youth delight, A little louder, but as empty quite; Scarfs, garters, gold, amuse his riper stage, And beads and prayer-books are the toys of age; Pleased with this bauble still, as that before; Till tired he sleeps, and life's poor play is o'er.

"AN ESSAY ON MAN"--Pope.

PROEM

THERE was a man.

And it happened--as such things often so happen--that this man went back into his days that were gone. Again and again and again he went back. Even as every man, even as you and I, so this man went back into his Yesterdays.

Then--why then there was a woman.

And it happened--as such things sometimes so happen--that this woman also went back into her days that were gone. Again and again and again she went back. Even as every woman, even as you and I, so this woman went back into her Yesterdays.

So it happened--as such things do happen--that the Yesterdays of this man and the Yesterdays of this woman became Their Yesterdays, and that they went back, then, no more alone but always together.

Even as one, they, forever after, went back.

What They Found in Their Yesterdays

And the man and the woman who went back into Their Yesterdays found there the Thirteen Truly Great Things of Life. Just as they found these things in their grown up days, even unto the end, so they found them in Their Yesterdays.

Thirteen Truly Great Things of Life there are. No life can

have less. No life can have more. All of life is in them. No life is without them all.

Dreams, Occupation, Knowledge, Ignorance, Religion, Tradition, Temptation, Life, Death, Failure, Success, Love, Memories: these are the Thirteen Truly Great Things of Life--found by the man and the woman in their grown up days--found by them in Their Yesterdays--and they found no others.

It does not matter where this man and this woman lived, nor who they were, nor what they did. It does not matter when or how many times they went back into Their Yesterdays. These things are all that they found. And they found these things even as every man and woman finds them, even as you and I find them, in our days that are and in our days that were--in our grown up days and in our Yesterdays.

And it is so that in all of these Thirteen Truly Great Things of Life there is a man and there is a woman.

DREAMS

The man, for the first time, stood face to face with Life and, for the first time, knew that he was a man.

For a long time he had known that some day he would be a man. But he had always thought of his manhood as a matter of years. He had said to himself: "when I am twenty-one, I will be a man." He did not know, then, that twenty-one years--that indeed three times twenty-one years--cannot make a man. He did not know, then, that men are made of other things than years.

I cannot tell you the man's name, nor the names of his parents, nor his exact age, nor just where he lived, nor any of those things. For my story, such things are of no importance whatever. But this is of the greatest importance: as the man, for the first time, stood face to face with Life and, for the first time, realized his manhood, his manhood life began in Dreams.

It is the dreams of life that, at the beginning of life, matter. Of the Thirteen Truly Great Things of Life, Dreams are first.

It was green fruit time. From the cherry tree that grew in the upper corner of the garden next door, close by the hedge that separated the two places, the blossoms were gone and the tiny cherries were already well formed. The nest, that a pair of little brown birds had made that spring in the hedge, was just empty, and, from the green laden branches of the tree, the little brown mother was calling anxious advice and sweet worried counsel to her sons and daughters who were trying their new wings.

In the cemetery on the hill, beside a grave over which the sod had formed thick and firm, there was now another grave--another grave so new that on it no blade of grass had started--so new that the yellow earth in the long rounded mound was still moist and the flowers that tried with such loving, tender, courage, to hide its nakedness were not yet wilted. Cut in the block of white marble that marked the grass-grown grave were the dearest words in any tongue--Wife and Mother; while, for the new-made mound that lay so close beside, the workmen were carving on a companion stone the companion words.

There were two other smaller graves nearby--one of them quite small--but they did not seem to matter so much to the tall young fellow who had said to himself so many times: "when I am twenty-one, I will be a man." It was the two graves marked by the companion words that mattered. And certainly he did not, at that time, feel himself a man. As he left the cemetery to go home with an old neighbor and friend of the family, he felt himself rather a very small and lonely boy in a very big and empty world.

But there had been many things to do in those next few days, with no one but himself to do them. There had been, in the voices of his friends, a note that was new. In the manner of the men who had come to talk with him on matters of business, he had felt a something that he had never felt before. And he had seen the auctioneer--a lifelong friend of his father--standing on the front porch of his boyhood home and had heard him cry the low spoken bids and answer the nodding heads of the buyers in a voice that was hoarse with something more than long speaking in the open air. And then--and then--at last had come the sharp blow of the hammer on the porch railing and from the trembling lips of the old auctioneer the word: "Sold."

It was as though that hammer had fallen on the naked heart of the boy. It was as though the auctioneer had shouted: "Dead."

And so the time had come, a week later, when he must go for a last look at the home that was his no longer. Very slowly he had walked about the yard; pausing a little before each tree and bush and plant; putting forth his hand, at times, to touch them softly as though he would make sure that they were there for he saw them dimly through a mist. The place was strangely hushed and still. The birds and bees and even the butterflies seemed to have gone somewhere far away. Very slowly he had gone up the steps to open the front door. Very slowly he had passed from room to room in the empty, silent, house. On the kitchen porch he had paused again, for a little, because he could not see the steps; then had gone on to the well, the garden, the woodhouse, the shop, the barn, and so out into the orchard that shaded the gently rising slope of the hill beyond the house. At the farther side of the orchard, on the brow of the hill, he had climbed the rail fence and had seated himself on the ground where he could look out and away over the familiar meadows and fields and pastures.

A bobo-link, swinging on a nearby bush, poured forth a tumbling torrent of silvery melody. Behind him, on the fence, a meadow lark answered with liquid music. About him on every side, in the soft sunlight, the bluebirds were flitting here and there, twittering cheerily the while over their bluebird tasks. And a woodpecker, hard at work in the orchard shade, made himself known by the din of his industry.

But the man, who did not yet quite realize that he was a man, gave no heed to these busy companions of his boyhood. To him, it was as though those men with their shovels had heaped that mound of naked, yellow, earth upon his heart. The world, for him, was as empty as the old house down there under the orchard hill. For a long time he sat very still--seeing nothing, hearing nothing, heeding nothing--conscious only of that dull, aching, loneliness--conscious only of that heavy weight of pain.

A mile or more away, beyond the fields, a moving column of smoke from a locomotive lifted itself into the sky above the tree tops and streamed back a long, dark, banner. As the column of smoke moved steadily on toward the distant horizon, the young man on the hilltop watched it listlessly. Then, as his mind outran the train to the cities that lay beyond the line of the sky, his eyes cleared, his countenance brightened, his thoughts went outward toward the great world where great men toil mightily; and the long, dark, banner of smoke that hung above the moving train became to him as a flag of battle leading swiftly toward the front. Eagerly now he watched--watched until, far away, the streaming column of smoke passed from sight around a wooded hill and faint and clear through the still air--a bugle call to his ears--came the long challenging whistle.

Then it was that he realized his manhood--knew that he was a man--and understood that manhood is not a matter of only twenty-one years. And then it was--as he sat there alone on the brow of the little hill with his boyhood years dead behind him and the years of his manhood before--that his manhood life began, even as the manhood life of every man really begins, with his Dreams.

Indeed it is true that all life really begins in dreams. Surely the lover dreams of his mistress--the maiden of her mate. Surely mothers dream of the little ones that sleep under their hearts and fathers plan for their children before they hold them in their arms. Every work of man is first conceived in the worker's soul and wrought out first in his dreams. And the wondrous world itself, with its myriad forms of life, with its grandeur, its beauty and its loveliness; the stars and the heavenly bodies of light that crown the universe; the marching of the days from the Infinite to the Infinite; the procession of the years from Eternity to Eternity; all this, indeed, is but God's good dream. And the hope of immortality--of that better life that lies beyond the horizon of our years--what a vision is that--what a wondrous dream--given us by God to inspire, to guide, to comfort, to hold us true!

With wide eyes the man looked out upon a wide world somewhat as a conquering emperor, confident in his armed strength, might from a hilltop look out over the scene of a coming battle. He did not see the grinding hardships, the desperate struggles, the disastrous losses, the pitiful suffering. The dreadful dangers did not grip his heart. The horrid fear of defeat did not strike his soul. He did not know the dragging weight of responsibility nor the dead weariness of a losing fight. He saw only the deeds of mighty valor, the glorious exhibitions of courage, of heroism, of strength. He felt only the thrill of victories, the pride of honors and renown. He knew only the inspiration of a high purpose. He heard only the call to greatness. And it was well that in his Dreams there were only these.

The splendid strength of young manhood stirred mightily in his limbs. The rich, red, blood of youth moved swiftly in his veins. His eager spirit shouted aloud in exultation of the deeds that he would do. And, surely, it was no shame to him that at this moment, when for the first time he realized his manhood, this man, in his secret heart, felt himself to be a leader of men, a conqueror of men, a savior of men. It was no shame to him that he felt the salvation of the world depending upon him.

And he was right. Upon him and upon such as he the salvation of the world *does* depend. But it is well, indeed, that these unrecognized, dreaming, saviors of the world do not know, as they dream, that their crosses, even then, are being prepared for them. It is their salvation that they do not know. It is the salvation of the world that they do not know.

And then, as one from the deck of a ship bound for a foreign land looks back upon his native shore when the vessel puts out from the harbor, this man turned from his years that were to come to his years that were past and from dreaming of his future slipped back into the dreams of his Yesterdays. Perhaps it was the song of the bobo-link that did it; or it may have been the music of the meadow lark; or perhaps it was the bluebird's cheerful notes, or the woodpecker's loud tattoo--whatever it was that brought it about, the man dreamed again the dreams of his boyhood--dreamed them even as he dreamed the dreams of his manhood.

And there was no one to tell him that, in dreaming, his boyhood and his manhood were the same.

Once again a boy, on a drowsy summer afternoon, he lay in the shade of the orchard trees or, in the big barn, sought the mow of new mown hay, and, with half closed eyes, slipped away from the world that droned and hummed and buzzed so lazily about him into another and better world of stirring adventure and brave deeds. Once again, when the sun was hidden under heavy skies and a steady pouring rain shut him in, through the dusk of the attic he escaped from the narrow restrictions of the house, and, from his gloomy prison, went out into a fairyland of romance, of knighthood, and of chivalry. Again it was winter time and the world was buried deep under white drifts, with all its brightness and beauty of meadow and forest hidden by the cold mantle, and all its music of running brooks and singing birds hushed by an icy hand, when, snug and warm under blankets and comforters, after an evening of stories, he slipped away into the wonderland of dreams--not the irresponsible, sleeping, dreams--those do not count--but the dreams that come between waking and sleeping, wherein a boy dare do all the great deeds he ever read about and can be all the things that ever were put in books for boys to wish they were.

Oh, but those were brave dreams--those dreams of his Yesterdays! No cruel necessity of life hedged them in. No wall of the practical or possible set a limit upon them. No right or wrong decreed the way they should go. In his Yesterdays, there were fairy Godmothers to endow him with unlimited power and to grant all his wishes, even unto mountains of golden wealth and vast caverns filled with all manner of precious gems. In his Yesterdays, there were wicked giants and horrid dragons and evil beasts to kill, with always a good Genii to see that they did not harm him the while he bravely took their baleful lives. In his Yesterdays, he was a prince in gorgeous raiment; an emperor with jeweled scepter and golden crown; a knight in armor, with a sword and proudly stepping horse of war; he was a soldier leading a forlorn hope; or a general, with his plumed staff officers about him, directing the battle from a mountain top; he was a sailor cast away on a desert island; or a captain commanding his ship in a storm or, clinging to the shrouds in a smother of battle flame and smoke, shouting his orders through a trumpet to his gallant crew; he was a pirate; a robber chief; a red Indian; a hunter; a scout of the plains--he could be anything, in those dreams of his Yesterdays, anything.

So, even as the man, the boy had dreamed. But the man did not think of it in that way--the dreams of his *manhood* were too real.

Then in his Yesterdays would come, also, the putting of his dreams into action, for the play of children, even as the works of men, are only dreams in action after all. The quiet orchard became a vast and pathless forest wherein lurked wild beasts and savage men ready to pounce upon the daring hunter; or, perhaps, it was an enchanted wood with lords and ladies imprisoned in the trees while in the carriage house--which was not a carriage house at all but a great castle--a cruel giant held captive their beautiful princess. The haymow was a robbers' cave wherein great wealth of booty was stored; the garden, a desert island on which lived the poor castaway. And many a long summer hour the bold captain clung to the rigging of his favorite apple tree ship and gazed out over the waving meadow sea, or the general of the army, on his rail fence war horse, directed the battle from the hilltop or led the desperate charge.

But rarely, in his Yesterdays, could the boy put his dreams into successful action alone. Alone he could dream but to realize his dreams, he needs must have the help of another. And so *she* came to take her place in his life, to help him play out his dreams--the little girl who lived next door.

Who was she? Why, she was the beautiful princess held captive by the giant in his carriage house castle until rescued by the brave prince who came to her through the enchanted wood. She was the crew of the apple tree ship; the robber band; the army following her general in his victorious charge; and the relief expedition that found the castaway on his desert island. Sometimes she was even a cannibal chief, or a monster dragon, or a cruel wild beast. And always--though the boy did not know--she was a good fairy weaving many spells for his happiness.

The man remembered well enough the first time that he met her. A new family was moving into the house that stood just below the garden and, from his seat on the gate post, the boy was watching the big wagons, loaded with household goods, as they turned into the neighboring yard. On the high seat of one of the wagons was the little girl. A big man lifted her down and the boy, watching, saw her run gaily into the house. For some time he held his place, swinging his bare legs impatiently, but he did not see the little girl come out into the yard again. Then, dropping to the ground, the boy slipped along the garden fence under the currant bushes to a small opening in the hedge that separated the two places. Very cautiously, at first, he peered through the branches. Then, upon finding all quiet, he grew bolder, and on hands and knees crept part way through the little green tunnel to find himself, all suddenly, face to face with her.

That was the beginning. The end had come several years later when the family had moved again.

The parting, too, he remembered well enough. A boy and girl parting it was. And the promises--boy and girl promises they were. At first many poorly written, awkwardly expressed, laboriously compiled, but warmly interesting letters were exchanged. Then the letters became shorter and shorter; the intervals between grew longer and longer; until, even as childhood itself goes, she had slipped out of his life. Even as the brave dreams of his boyhood she had gone--even as his Yesterdays.

The bobo-link had long ago left his swinging bush. The meadow lark had gone to find his mate in a distant field. The twittering bluebirds had finished their tasks. The woodpecker had ceased from his labor. The sunshine was failing fast. Faint and far away, through the still twilight air, came the long, clear, whistle of another train that was following swiftly the iron ways to the world of men.

The man on the hill came back from his Yesterdays--came back to wonder: "where is the little girl now? Has she changed much? Her eyes would be the same and her hair--only a little darker perhaps. And does she ever go back into the Yesterdays? It is not likely," he thought, "no doubt she is far too busy caring for her children and attending to her household duties to think of her childhood days and her childhood playmate. And what would her husband be like?" he wondered.

There was no woman in the dreams of the man who that afternoon, for the first time, realized his manhood and began his manhood life. He dreamed only of the deeds that he would do; of the work he would accomplish; of the place he would win; and of the honors he would receive. The little girl lived for him only in his Yesterdays. She did not belong to his manhood years. She had no place in his manhood dreams.

Slowly he climbed the rail fence again and, through the orchard, went down the hill toward the house. But he did not again enter the house. He went on past the kitchen porch to the garden gate where he stood, for some minutes, looking toward the hedge that separated the two places and toward the cherry tree that grew in the corner of the garden next door.

At the big front gate he paused again and turned lingeringly as one reluctant to go. The old home in the twilight seemed so lonely, so deserted by all to whom it had been most kind.

At last, with a movement suggestive of a determination that could not have belonged to his boyhood, he set his face toward the world. Down the little hill in the dusk of the evening he went, walking quickly; past the house where the little girl had lived; across the creek at the foot of the hill; and on up the easy rise beyond. And, as he went, there was on his face the look of a man. There was in his eyes a new light--the light of a man's dream. Nor did he once look back.

To-morrow he would leave the friends of his boyhood; he would leave the scenes of his Yesterdays; he would go to work out his dreams--even as in his Yesterdays, he would play them out--for the works of men are as the plays of children but dreams in action, after all.

Would he, *could* he, play out his manhood dreams alone?

And the woman also, for the first time, was face to face with Life and, for the first time, knew that she was a woman.

For a long while she had seen her womanhood approaching. Little by little, as her skirts had been lengthened, as her dolls had been put away, as her hair had been put up, she had seen her womanhood drawing near. But she had always said to herself: "when I do not play with dolls, when I can dress like mother, and fix my hair like mother, I will be a woman." She did not know, then, that womanhood is a matter of things very different from these. Until that night she did not know. But that night she knew.

I cannot tell you the woman's name, nor where she lived, nor any of those things that are commonly told about women in stories. But, as my story is not that kind of a story, it will not matter that I cannot tell. What really matters to my story is this: the woman, that night, when, for the first time, she knew herself to be a woman, began her woman life in dreams. Because the dreams of life are of the greatest importance--because Dreams are of the Thirteen Truly Great Things of Life--this is my story: that the woman life of this woman, when first she knew herself to be a woman, began in dreams.

It was the time of the first roses. For a week or more she had been very busy with a loving, tender, joyous, occupation that left her no time to think of herself. Her dearest friend--her girlhood's most intimate companion, and, save for herself, the last of their little circle--was to be married and she was to be bridesmaid.

They had been glad days--those days of preparation--for she rejoiced greatly in the happiness of her friend and had shared, as fully as it was possible for another to share, the sweet sacredness, the holy mysteriousness, and the proud triumph of it all. But with the gladness of those days, there had come into her heart a strange quietness like the quietness of an empty room that is furnished and ready but without a tenant.

At the wedding that evening she had been all that a bridesmaid should be, even to the last white ribbon and the last handful of rice, for she would that no shadow of a cloud should come over the happiness of her friend. But when the new-made husband and wife had been put safely aboard the Pullman, and, with the group on the depot platform frantically waving hats and handkerchiefs and shouting good lucks and farewells, the train had pulled away, the loneliness in her heart had become too great to hide. Her escort had made smart jokes about her tears, alleging disappointment and envy. He was a poor, shallow, witless, fool who could not understand; and that he could not understand mattered, to her, not at all. She had commanded him to take her home and at her front door had thanked him and sent him away.

And then it was--in the blessed privacy of her own room, with the door locked and the shades drawn close, with her wedding finery thrown aside and the need of self-repression no longer imperative--that, as she sat in a low chair before the fire, she looked, for the first time, boldly at Life and, for the first time, knew that she was a woman--knew that womanhood was not a matter of long skirts, of hair dressing, and the putting away of dolls.

She was tired, very tired, from the responsibilities and excitement of the day but she did not feel that she could sleep. From the fire, she looked up to the clock that ticked away so industriously on the mantle. It was a little clock with a fat, golden, cupid grasping the dial in his chubby arms as though striving to do away with time when he might better have been busy with his bow and arrows. The hands of the clock pointed nearly midnight. The young woman looked into the fire again.

Already her girl friend had been a wife several hours--a wife.

Already the train was miles away bearing the newly wedded ones to their future home--their home. The hours would go swiftly into days, the days into weeks and months and years, and there would be boys and girls--their children. And the years would go swiftly as the days and there would be the weddings of their sons and daughters and then--the children of their children.

And the woman who that night knew that she was a woman--the woman whose heart, as she sat alone before the fire, was even as an empty room--a room that is furnished and ready but without a tenant--what, this woman asked herself, would the years bring her? The years of her childhood and girlhood were past. What of her womanhood years that were to come?

There are many doors in the life of these modern days at which a woman may knock with hope of being admitted; and this woman, as she sat alone before her fire that night, paused before them all--all save two. Two doors she saw but did not pause before; and *one* of them was idleness and pleasure. And one other door there is that stands open wide so that there is no need to knock for admittance. Before this wide open door the woman paused a long time. It is older than the other doors. It is very, very, old. Since the beginning it has never been closed. But though it stood open so wide and there was no need to knock for admittance, still the woman could not enter for she was alone. No woman may enter that old, old, open door, alone.

Three times before she had stood before that ancient door and had been urged to cross the threshold; but always she had hesitated, had held back, and turned away. She wondered if always she would hesitate, if always she would turn away; or would some one come with whom she could gladly, joyously, confidently, cross the threshold. She could not say. She could only wait. And while she waited she would knock at one of the other doors. She would knock because she must. The custom of the age, necessity, circumstances, forced her to knock at one of those doors that, in the life of these modern days, opens to women who seek admittance alone.

I cannot tell just what the circumstances of the woman's life were nor why it was necessary. Nor does it in the least matter that I cannot tell. The necessity, the circumstances, have nothing to do with my story save this: that, whatever they were, I am quite sure they ought not to have been. I am quite sure that *any* circumstance, or necessity, or custom, that forces a woman who knows herself to be a woman to seek admittance at any one of those doors through which she must enter alone is not right. This it is that belongs to my story: the woman did not wish to enter the life that lies on the other side of those doors through which she must go alone.

Alone in her room that night, with the shades drawn close and the only light the light of the dancing fire, this woman who, for the first time, knew herself to be a woman, did not dream of a life on the other side of those doors at which she must ask admittance. She dreamed of a future beyond the old, old, door that has stood open wide since the beginning.

And it was no shame to her that she so dreamed. It was no shame that she called before her, one by one, those who had asked her to cross with them the threshold and those who might still ask her. It was no shame that, while her heart said always, "no," she still waited--waited for one whom she knew not but only knew that she would know him when he came. And it was no shame to her that, even while this was so, she saw herself in the years to come a wife and mother. In the glowing heart of the fire she saw her home warm with holy love, bright with sacred companionship. In the dancing flames she saw her children--happy, beautiful, children. Nor did she in her dreams fear the flickering shadows that came and went for in the dusk of the room she felt the dear presence of that one who was to be her other self; who was to be to her strength in her weakness, hope in her sadness, and comfort in her mourning.

It is well indeed that the shadows of life bring no fears into our dreams else we would not dare to dream and life itself would lose its purpose and its meaning.

So the woman saw her future, not in the shadows that came and went upon the wall, but in the glowing heart of the fire. And, as she dreamed her dreams of womanhood, her face grew beautiful with a tender, thoughtful, beauty that is given only to those women who dream such dreams. With the realization of her womanhood and the beginning of her woman life, her lips curved in a smile that was different from the smile of girlhood and there came into her eyes a light that was never there before. And then, as one setting out on a long journey might turn back for a last farewell view of loved familiar scenes, she turned to go back for a little into her Yesterdays.

There was a home in those Yesterdays and there was a mother--a mother who lived now in a better home than any of earth's building. A father she had never known but there was a big, jolly, uncle who had done and was doing yet all that an uncle of limited means could do to take her father's place in the life of his sister's only child. And there was sunshine in her Yesterdays--bright sunshine--unclouded by city smoke; and flowers unstained by city grime; and blue skies unmarred by city buildings; and there were beautiful trees and singing birds and broad fields in her Yesterdays. Also there were dreams--such dreams as only those who are very young or very wise dare to dream.

It may have been the firelight that did it; it may have been the vision of her children who lived only in the life that she saw beyond the old, old, open door: or perhaps it was the wedding finery that lay over a nearby chair: or the familiar tick, tick, tick, of the clock in the arms of the fat cupid who neglected his bow and arrows in a vain attempt to do away with time--whatever it was that brought it about, the woman dreamed again the dreams of childhood--dreamed them even as she dreamed those first dreams of her womanhood.

And no one was there to tell her that the dreams of her girlhood and of her womanhood were the same.

Again, on a long summer afternoon, as she kept house in a snug corner of the vine shaded porch, she was really the mistress of a grand mansion that was furnished with beautiful carpets and furniture, china and silver, books and pictures. And in that mansion she received her distinguished guests and entertained her friends with charming grace and dignity, even as she set her tiny play table with dishes of thimble size and served tea and cakes to her play lady friends. Again, as she rocked her dollies to sleep beside the evening fire and tucked them into their beds with a little mother kiss for each, there were dreams of merry boys and girls who should some day call her mother. And there were dreams of fine dresses and jewels the while she stitched tiny garments for her newest child who had come to her with no clothing at all, or fashioned a marvelous hat for another whose features were but a smudge of paint and whose hair had been glued on so many times that it was far past combing and a hat was a necessity to hide the tangled mat. And sometimes she was a princess shut up in a castle tower and a noble prince, who wore golden armor and rode a great war horse, would come to woo her and she would ride away with him through the deep forest followed by a long procession of lords and ladies, of knights and squires and pages. Or, perhaps, she would be a homeless girl in pitiful rags who, because of her great beauty, would be stolen by gypsies and sold to a cruel king to be kept in a dungeon until rescued by a brave soldier lover.

And, in her Yesterdays, the master of the dream home over which she was mistress--the father of her dream children--the prince with whom she rode away through the forest--the soldier lover who rescued her from the dungeon--and the hero of many other adventures of which she was the heroine--was always the same. Outside her dreams he was a sturdy, brown cheeked, bare legged, little boy who lived next door. But what a man is outside a woman's dreams counts for little after all--even though that woman be a very small and dainty little woman with a very large family of dolls.

The woman remembered so well their first meeting. It was at the upper end of the garden near the strawberry beds and he was creeping toward her on hands and knees through a hole in the hedge that separated the two places. How she had jumped when she first caught sight of him! How he had started and turned as if to escape when he saw her watching him! How shyly they had approached each other with the first timid offerings of friendship!

Many, many, times after that did he come to her through the opening in the hedge. Many, many, times did she go to him. And he came in many disguises. In many disguises she helped him put his dreams into action. But always, to her, he was a hero to be worshiped, a leader to be followed, a master to be obeyed. Always she was very proud of him--of his strength and courage--of the grand deeds he wrought--and of the great things that he would some day do. And sometimes--the most delightful times of all--at her wish, he would help her, in his masterful way, to play out her dreams. And then, though he liked being an Indian or a robber or a soldier best, he would be a model husband and help her with the children; although he did, at times, insist upon punishing them rather more than she thought necessary. But when the little family was ill with the measles or scarlet fever or whooping cough no dream husband could have been more gentle, more thoughtful, or more wise, in his attention.

And once they had played a wedding.

The woman whose heart was as an empty room stirred in her chair uneasily as one who feels the gaze of a hidden observer. But the door was locked, the shades drawn close, and the only light was the flickering light of the fire. The night without was very dark and still. There was no sound in the sleeping house-- no sound save the steady tick, tick, tick, of the time piece in the chubby arms of the fat cupid on the mantle.

And once they had played a wedding.

It was when her big, jolly, uncle was married. The boy and the girl were present at the ceremony and she wore a wonderful new dress while the boy, scrubbed and combed and brushed, was arrayed in his best clothes with shoes and stockings. There were flowers and music and good things to eat and no end of laughter and gay excitement; and the jolly uncle looked so big and fine and solemn; and the bride, in her white veil, was so like a princess in one of the dreams; that the little girl was half frightened and felt a queer lump in her throat as she clung to her mother's hand. And there was a strange ceremony in which the minister, in his gown, read out of a book and said a prayer and asked questions; and the uncle and the princess answered the questions; and the uncle put a ring on the finger of the princess; and the minister said that they were husband and wife. And then there were kisses while everybody laughed and cried and shook hands; and some one told the little girl that the princess was her new auntie; and her uncle caught her up in his big arms and was his own jolly self again. It was all very fine and strange and impressive to their childish eyes; and so, of course, the very next day, the boy and the girl played a wedding.

It was up in that quiet corner of the garden, near the hedge, and the cherry tree was in bloom and showered its delicate blossoms down upon them with every puff of air that stirred the branches; while, in the hedge nearby, a little brown bird was putting the finishing touch to a new nest. The boy's shepherd dog, who sat up when you told him, was the minister; and all the dollies were there, dressed in their finest gowns. The little girl was very serious and again, half frightened, felt that queer lump in her throat as she promised to be his wife. And the boy looked very serious, too, as he placed a little brass ring upon her finger and, speaking for the brown eyed, shaggy coated, minister, said: "I pronounce you husband and wife and anything that God has done must never be done any different by anybody forever and ever, Amen." And then--because there was no one else present and they both felt that the play would not be complete without-- then, he had kissed her, and they were both very, very, happy.

So it was that, in the quiet secrecy of her dimly lighted room, the woman who that night knew herself to be a woman, felt her cheeks hot with blushes and upon her hot cheeks felt her tears.

So it was that she came back from her Yesterdays to wonder: where was the boy now? What kind of a man had he grown to be? Was he making his way to fame and wealth or laboring in some humble position? Had he a home with wife and children? Did he ever go back into the Yesterdays? Had he forgotten that wedding under the cherry tree? When the one with whom she would go through the old, old, door into the life of her womanhood dreams should come, would it matter if the hero of her childhood dreams went in with them? He could be no rival to that one who was to come for he lived only in the Yesterdays and the Yesterdays could not come back. The fat little cupid on the mantle neglected his bow and arrows in vain; he could not do away with time.

Very slowly the woman prepared for her rest and, when she was ready, knelt in the soft dusk of her room, a virgin in white to pray. And God, I know, understood why her prayer was confused and uncertain with longings she could not express even to him who said: "Except ye become as little children." God, I know, understood why this woman, who that night, for the first time, knowing herself to be a woman had dreamed a true woman's dream--God, I know, understood why, as she lay down to sleep in the quiet darkness, she stretched forth her empty arms and almost cried aloud.

In to-morrow's light it would all be gone, but that night--that night--her womanhood dreams of the future were real--real even as the girlhood dreams of her Yesterdays.

OCCUPATION

IN a small, bare, room in a cheap city boarding house, the man cowered like a wild thing, wounded, neglected, afraid; while over him, gaunt and menacing, cruel, pitiless, insistent, stood a dreadful need--the need of Occupation--the need of something to do.

In all the world there is no danger so menacing as the danger of idleness: there is no privation so cruel, no suffering so pitiful, as the need of Occupation: there is no demand so imperative, no necessity so dreadful, as the want of something to do.

Occupation is the very life of Life. As nature abhors a vacuum so life abhors idleness. To *be* is to be occupied. Even though one spend his days in seeking selfish pleasures still must he occupy himself to live, for the need of something to do is most imperative upon those who strive hardest to do nothing. As life and the deeds of men are born in dreams so life itself is Occupation. A man *is* the thing he does. What the body is to the spirit; what the word is to the thought; what the sunshine is to the sun; Occupation is to Dreams. One of the Thirteen Truly Great Things of Life is Occupation.

From the cherry tree in the upper corner of the garden near the hedge, the cherries had long ago been gathered. The pair of brown birds had reared their children and were beginning to talk with their neighbors and kinfolk about their winter home in the south. In the orchard on the hill back of the house, the late fruit was hanging, full ripe, upon the bending boughs. From the brow of the hill, where the man had sat that afternoon when, for the first time, he faced Life and knew that he was a man, the fields from which the ripened grain had been cut lay in the distance, great bars and blocks and patches of golden yellow, among the still green pastures and meadows and the soft brown strips of the fall plowing. In the woods, the squirrels were beginning to take stock of the year's nut crop and to make their estimates for the winter's need, preparing, the while, their storehouses to receive the precious hoard. And over that new mound in the cemetery, the grass fairies had woven a coverlid thick and firm and fine as though, in sweet pity of its yellow nakedness, they would shield it from the winds that already had in them a hint that summer's reign was past.

But all this was far, very far, from where, in his small bare room, the man crouched frightened and dismayed. The rush and roar of the crowded trains on the elevated road outside his window shook the casement with impatient fury. The rumbling thunder of the heavily loaded subway trains jarred the walls of the building. The rattle and whirr of the overflowing surface cars rose sharply above the hum and din of the city streets. To the man who asked only a chance, only a place, only room to stand and something-- anything--to do, it was maddening. A blind, impotent, fury took possession of him. He clenched his fists and cursed aloud.

But the great, crowded, world heeded his curses as little as it noticed him and he fell again into the silence of his hopelessness.

Out from the sheltered place of his dreams the man had come into the busy world of deeds--into the world where those who, like himself, had dreamed, were putting their dreams into action. Out from the years of his boyhood he had come into the years of his manhood--out from the scenes of his Yesterdays into the scenes of his to-days.

For weeks, with his young strength stirring mightily within him and his rich, red, blood hot in his veins, he had been crying out to the world: "Make way for me. Give me a place that I may work out my dreams. Give me something to do." For weeks, he had been trying to convince the world that it needed him. But the busy, happy, world--the idle, dreaming, world--the discontented, sullen, world--was not so easily convinced. His young strength and his red blood did not seem to count for as much as they should. His confidence and his courage did not seem to impress. His high rank in the boyhood world did not entitle him to a like position among men. His graduating address had made no stir in the world of thought. His athletic record had caused no comment in the world of industry. His coming did not disturb the world of commerce.

A few he found who wrought with all the vigor and enthusiasm of their dreaming. These said: "What have you done that we should make room for you? Prove yourself first then come to us." Many he saw who had wearied of the game and were dreaming new dreams. These said: "We ourselves are without Occupation. There are not places enough for all. Stand aside and give us room." Many others there were who, with dreams forgotten, labored as dull cattle, goaded by brute necessity, with no vision, no purpose, no hope, to make of their toil a blessing. And these laughed at him with vicious laughter, saying: "Why should anyone want anything to do?"

So the man in those days saw his dreams going from him--saw his bright visions growing dim. So he came to feel that his young strength was of no value; that his red blood was worthless; that his courage was vain. So his confidence was shaken; his faith was weakened; his hope grew faint. He came to feel that the things that he had dreamed were already all wrought out--that there were no more great works to be done--that all that could be done was being accomplished--that in all the world there was nothing more for a man to do. Disappointed, discouraged, disheartened, weary and alone, he told himself that he had come too late--that in all the world there was nothing more for a man to do.

He did not look out upon the world, now, as a conquering emperor, confident in his armed strength, might look over the field of a coming battle. He did not dream, now, of victories, of honors, and renown. He did not, now, see himself a savior of the world. The world had stretched this man also upon the cross that it has always ready for such as he.

It was not the man's pressing need that hurt him so--gladly he would have suffered for his dreams. It was not for privation and hardships that he cared--proudly he would have endured those for his dreams. Nor was it loneliness and neglect that made him afraid--he was willing to work out his dreams alone. That which sent him cowering like a wounded, wild thing to his room was this: he felt that his strength, his courage, his willingness, his purpose, were as nothing in the world. That which frightened him with dreadful fear was this: he felt that his dreams were going from him. That for which he cared was this: he felt that he was too late. This was the cross upon which the world stretched him--the cross of enforced idleness--the cross of *nothing to do*.

It is not strange that in his lonely suffering the man sought to escape by the only way open to him--the way that led to his Yesterdays. There was a welcome for him there. There was a place for him. He was wanted there. There his life was held of value. It is not at all strange that he went back. As one flees from a desolate, burning, desert waste, to a land of shady groves and fruitful gardens, of cool waters and companionable friends, so this man fled from his days that were into his days that were gone--so he went back into his Yesterdays.

It may have been the soft dusk of the twilight hour that did it: or it may have been the loneliness of his heart: or, perhaps, it was the picture he found in his trunk as he searched among his few things trying to decide what next he should take to the pawn shop. Whatever it was that brought it about, the man was a boy again in the boyhood world of his Yesterdays.

And it happened that the day in his Yesterdays to which the man went back was one of those days when the boy could find nothing to do. Every game that he had ever played was played out. Every source of amusement he had exhausted. There was in all his boyhood world nothing, nothing, for him to do.

The orchard was not a trackless forest inhabited by fierce, wild beasts; nor an enchanted wood with lords and ladies imprisoned in the trees; it was only an orchard--a commonplace old orchard--nothing more. Indians and robbers were stupid creatures of no importance whatever. There were no fairies, no giants, no soldiers left in the boyhood world. The rail fence war horse refused to charge. The apple tree ship was a wreck on the rocks of discontent. The hay had all been cut and stored away in the barn. The excitement and fun of the grain harvesting was over and the big stacks were waiting the threshers. It was not time for fall apple picking and the cider mill, nor to gather the corn, nor to go nutting. There was nothing, nothing, to do.

The boy's father was busy with some sort of work in the shop and told his little son not to bother. The hired man was doing something to the barnyard fence and told the boy to get out of the way. A carpenter was repairing the roof of the house and the long ladder looked inviting enough, but, the instant the boy's head appeared above the eaves, the man shouted for him to get down and to run and play. Even the new red calf refused to notice him but continued its selfish, absorbing, occupation with wobbly legs braced wide and tail wagging supreme indifference. His very dog had deserted him and had gone away somewhere on business of his own, apparently forgetting the needs of his master. And mother--mother too was busy, as busy as could be with sweeping and dusting and baking and mending and no end of things that must be done.

But somehow mother's work could always wait. At least it could wait long enough for her to look lovingly down into the troubled, discontented, little face while she listened to the plaintive whine: "There's nothin' at all to do. Mamma, tell me--tell me something to do."

Poor little boy in the Yesterdays! Quickly mother's arm went around him. Lovingly she drew him close. And mother's work waited still as she considered the serious problem. There was no feeling of not being wanted in the boy's heart then. As he looked up at her he felt already renewed hope and quickening interest.

Then mother's face brightened, in a way that mother faces do, and the boy's eyes began to shine in eager anticipation. What should he do? Why mother knew the very thing of course. It was the best--the very best--the most interesting thing in all the world for a boy to do. He should build a house for the little girl who lived next door.

Out under the lilac bushes he should build it, in a pretty corner of the yard, where mother, from her window, every now and then, could look out to see how well he was doing and help, perhaps, with careful suggestions. Mother herself would ask the carpenter man for some clean, new boards, some shingles and some nails. And it would all be a secret, between just mother and the boy, until the house was finished and ready and then he should go and bring the little girl and they would see how surprised and glad she would be.

It was wondrous magic those mothers worked in the Yesterdays. In a twinkle, for the boy who could find nothing to do, the world was changed. In a twinkle, there was nothing in all the world worth doing save this one thing--to build a house for the little girl next door.

With might and main he planned and toiled and toiled and planned; building and rebuilding and rebuilding yet again. He cut his fingers and pounded his thumb and stuck his hands full of slivers and minded it not at all so absorbed was he in this best of all Occupations.

But keep it secret! First there was father's smiling face close beside mother's at the window. Then the hired man chanced to pass and paused a moment to make admiring comment. And, later, the carpenter man came around the corner of the house and, when he saw, offered a bit of professional advice and voluntarily contributed another board. Even the boy's dog, as though he had heard the news that the very birds were discussing so freely in the tree tops, came hurrying home to manifest his interest. Keep it secret! How *could* the boy keep it secret! But the little girl did not know. Until he was almost ready to tell her, the little girl did not know. Almost he was ready to tell her, when--But that belongs to the other part of my story.

About the man in his bare, lonely, room in the great city, the world in its madness raged--struggling, pushing, crowding, jostling, scrambling--a swirling, writhing, mass of life--but the man did not heed. On every side, this life went rushing, roaring, rumbling, thundering, whirring, shrieking, clattering by. But the man noticed the world now no more than it noticed him. In his Yesterdays he had found something to do. He had found the only thing that a man, who knows himself to be a man, can do in truth to his manhood. Again, in his Yesterdays, he was building a house for the little girl who lived next door--the little girl who did not know.

Someday this childish old world will grow weary of its games of war and wealth. Someday it will lose interest in its playthings--banks, and stocks, and markets. Someday it will lose faith in its fairies of fame, its giants of position and power. Then will the disconsolate, forlorn, old world turn to Mother Nature to learn from her that the only Occupation that is of real and lasting worth is the one Occupation in which all of Mother Nature's children have fellowship--the Occupation of home building.

In meadow and forest and field; in garden and grove and

hedge and bush; in mountain and plain and desert and sea; in hollow logs; amid swaying branches; in rocky dens and earthy burrows; high among towering cliffs and mighty crags; low in the marsh grass and among reeds and rushes; in stone walls; in fence corners; in tufts of grass and tiny shrubs; among the flowers and swinging vines; everywhere--everywhere--in all this great, round, world, Mother's children all are occupied in home building--occupied in this and nothing more. This is the one thing that Mother's children, in all the ages since the beginning, have found worth doing. One wayward child alone is occupied just now, seemingly, with everything *but* home building. Man seems to be doing everything these days but the one thing that must be the foundation work of all. But never mind--homebuilding will be the world's work at the last. When all the playthings of childhood and all the childish games of men have failed, homebuilding will endure. Occupation must in the end mean home building or it is meaningless.

And the din, the confusion, the struggle, the turmoil of life--when it all means to men the building of homes and nothing more; when the efforts of men, the ambitions of men, the labor and toil of men are all to make homes for the little girls next door; then, will Mother Nature smile upon her boys and God, I am sure, will smile upon them, too.

The man came back from his Yesterdays with a new heart, with new courage and determination, and the next day he found something to do.

I do not know what it was that the man found to do--*that* is not my story.

* * * * *

It was nearly the time of falling leaves when the woman, who knew herself to be a woman, knocked at one of those doors, at which she did not wish to knock, and was admitted.

It does not matter which of the doors it was. I cannot tell you what work it was that the woman found to do. What mattered to her--and to the world if only the world would understand--was this: that she was forced by the customs of the age and by necessity to enter a life that her woman heart did not desire. While her dreams were of the life that lies beyond the old, old, door that has stood open since the beginning; while she waited on the threshold and longed to go in; she was forced to turn aside, to seek admittance at one of those other doors. This it is that matters--matters greatly. Perhaps only God who made the woman heart and who Himself set that door open wide--perhaps only God knows how greatly it matters.

Of course, if the woman had not known herself to be a woman, it would have made little difference either to her or to the world.

And the woman when she had joined that great company of women, who, in these modern days labor behind the doors through which they must go alone, found them to be good women--good and brave and true. And most of them, she found, were in that great company of workers just as she was there--just as every woman who knows her womanhood is there--through circumstances, the custom of the age, necessity. The only saving thing about it all is this: their woman hearts are somewhere else.

And the woman found also that, while the door opened readily enough to her knock, she was received without a welcome. Through that other door, the door that God himself has opened, she would have entered into a joyous welcome--she would have been received with gladness, with rejoicing, with holiest love, and highest honor. To her, in the world that lies beyond the old, old, door, would have been rendered homage and reverence second only to that given to God Himself. There, she would have been received as a *woman for her* womanhood; she would have been given first place among all created things. But the world into which she entered alone did not so receive her. It received her coldly. Its manner said quite plainly: "Why are you here? What do you want?" It said: "There is no sentiment here, no love, no reverence, no homage; there is only business here, only law, only figures and facts."

This world was not unkind to her, but it did not receive her as a woman. It could not. It did not value her *womanhood*. Womanhood has no value there. It valued her clear brain, her physical strength, her skillful hands, her willing feet, her ready wit: but her womanhood it ignored. The most priceless gift of the Creator to his creatures--the one thing without which all human effort would be in vain, no Christian prayer would be possible; the one thing without which mankind would perish from the earth-- this world, into which the woman went, rejected. But the things that belonged to her womanhood--the charm of her manner; the beauty of her face and form; the appeal of her sex; the quick intuitions of her soul--all these this world received and upon them put a price. They became not forces to be used by her in wifehood and motherhood but commercial assets, valued in dollars, worth a certain price upon the woman labor market in the business world.

And the woman's heart, because she knew herself to be a woman, rebelled at this buying and selling the things of her womanhood. These things she rightly felt to be above price--far, far, above price. They were the things of her wifehood and motherhood. They were given her to be used by her in love, in mating, in bearing and rearing children, in the giving of life to the world.

The things of a woman's womanhood are as far above price as life itself to which they belong. Even as color and perfume belong to the flowers; even as the music of the birds belongs to the feathery songsters; even as the blue belongs to the sky, and the light to the stars; so these graces of a woman belong to her and to the mission of her womanhood are sacred. They are hers to be used in her holy office of womanhood; by her alone, without price, for the glory and honor of life and the future of the race. So the woman's heart rebelled, but secretly, instinctively, almost unconsciously. Open rebellion would have made it impossible for her to remain in the world into which she entered because of her necessity and the custom of the age.

She found, too, that this world into which she had entered was very courteous, that it was even considerate and kind--as considerate and kind as it was possible to be--for it seemed to understand her position quite as well as she herself understood it. And this world paid her very well for the services she was asked to render. But it asked of her no favors. It accorded her no honors. It sought her with no offering. And, because of this, the woman, in the heart of her womanhood, felt ashamed and humiliated.

It is the right of womanhood to bestow favors. It is a woman's right to be honored above all creatures of earth. Since the beginning of life itself her sex has been so honored--has received the offerings from life. Mankind, alone, has at times attempted to change this law but has never quite succeeded. Mankind never can fully succeed in this because woman holds life itself in her keeping. So the woman felt that her womanhood was humiliated and shamed. But she hid this feeling also, hid it carefully, buried it deeply, because she knew that if she did not it would betray her and she would not be permitted to remain in the world into which necessity forced her. To the woman, it seemed that the world into which she had gone, itself, felt her shame and humiliation. That, in secret, it desired to ask of her; to accord to her honors; to seek her with offerings. But this world could not do these things because it dared not recognize her womanhood. When a woman goes into that world into which she must go alone, she leaves her womanhood behind. Her womanhood is not received there.

But most of all, the thing that troubled the woman was this: the risk she ran in entering into that life behind the door at which she had sought admittance. She saw that there was danger there--grave danger--to her womanhood. In the busy, ceaseless, activity of that life there would be little time for her waiting beside the old, old, door. The exacting demands of her work, or profession, or calling, or business, would leave little leisure for the meditation and reflection that is so large a part of the preparation necessary for entrance into that other world of which she had dreamed. Constant contact with the unemotional facts and figures of that life which sets a market value upon the sacred things of womanhood would make it ever more difficult for her to dream of love. There was grave danger that interest and enthusiasm in other things would supplant her longing for wifehood and motherhood. She feared that in her Occupation she might not know, when he came, that one who was to cross the threshold with her into the life of her dreams--that, indeed, he might come and go again while she was busy with other things. She feared that she would come to accept the commercial valuation of the things that belonged to her womanhood and thus forget their higher, holier, use and that the continued rejection of her womanhood would, in time, lead her to think of it lightly, as incidental rather than supreme. There was real danger that she would lose her desire to be sought, to give, to receive offerings; that she would cease to rebel secretly; that she would no longer feel humiliated at her position. She feared in short this danger--the gravest danger to her womanhood and thus to all that womankind holds in her keeping--that she would come to feel contented, satisfied, and happy, in being a part of the world into which she was forced to go by the custom of the age and by necessity. Because this woman knew herself to be a woman she feared this. If she had not come to know her womanhood she would not have feared it. Neither would it have mattered.

The woman was thinking of these things that Saturday afternoon as she walked homeward from her work. She often walked to her home on Saturday afternoons, when there was time, for she was strong and vigorous, with an abundance of good red woman blood in her veins, and loved the free movement in the open air.

Perhaps, though, it is not exact to say that she was *thinking* of these things. The better word would be *feeling*. She was not thinking of them as I have set them down: but she was feeling them all. She was conscious of them, just as she was conscious of the dead brown leaves that drifted across her path, though she was not thinking of the leaves. She felt them as she felt the breath of fall in the puff of air that drifted the leaves: but she did not put what she felt into words. So seldom do the things that women feel get themselves put into words.

The young woman had chosen a street that led in the direction of her home through one of the city's smaller parks, and, as she went, the people she met turned often to look after her for she was good to look at. She walked strongly but with a step as light as it was firm and free; and, breathing deeply with the healthful exercise, her cheeks were flushed with rosy color, her eyes shone, her countenance--her every glance and movement--betrayed a strong and perfect womanhood--a womanhood that, rightly understood, is wealth that the race and age can ill afford to squander.

Coming to the park, she walked more slowly and, after a little, seated herself on a bench to watch the squirrels that were playing nearby. The foliage had already lost its summer freshness though here and there a tree or bush made brave attempt to retain its garb of green. Not a few brown leaves whirled helplessly about--the first of unnumbered myriads that soon would be offered by the dying summer in tribute to winter's conquering power. The sun was still warm but the air had in it a subtle flavor that seemed a blending of the coming season with the season that was almost gone.

Near the farther entrance to the little park, a carpenter was repairing the roof of a house and, from where she sat, the woman could see the long ladder resting against the eaves. A boy with his shepherd dog came romping along the walk under the trees as irresponsible as the drifting leaves. The squirrels scampered away; the boy and dog whirled on; and the woman, from the world into which she had entered because she must, went far away into the world of childhood. From her day of toil in a world that denied her womanhood she went back into her Yesterdays where womanhood--motherhood--was supreme. Perhaps it was that subtle flavor in the air that did it; or it may have been the boy and his dog as they whirled past--care free as the drifting brown leaves; or perhaps it was the sight of the man repairing the roof of the house with his long ladder resting against the eaves: the woman herself could not have told what it was, but, whatever it was, she slipped away to one of the brightest, happiest, days in all her Yesterdays.

But, for a little while, that day was not at all bright and happy. It started out all right then, little by little, everything went wrong; and then it changed again and became one of the best of all her Yesterdays. The day went wrong for a little while at first because everything in the house was being taken up, or taken down, beaten, shaken, scrubbed or dusted; everything was being arranged or disarranged and rearranged again. Surely there was never such confusion, so it seemed to the little girl, in any home in all the world. Every time that she would get herself nicely settled with her dolls she would be forced to move again; until there was in the whole, busy, bustling place no corner at all where she was not in somebody's way. When she would have entered into the confusion and helped to straighten things out, the woman told her, rather sharply, to go away, and declared that her efforts to help only made things worse.

Out in the garden, at the opening in the hedge, she called

and called and waited and waited for the boy. But the boy did not answer. He was too busy, she thought, to care about her. She felt quite sure that he did not even want her to help in whatever it was that he was doing. Perhaps, she thought wistfully, peering through the little green tunnel, perhaps if she could go and find him he might--when he saw how miserable and lonely she was--he might be kind. But to go through the hedge was forbidden, except when mother said she might.

Sorrowfully she turned away to seek the kitchen where the cook was busy with the week's baking. But the cook, when the little girl offered to roll the pie crust or stir the frosting for the cake, was hurried and cross and declared that the little girl could not help but only hinder and that it would be better for her not to get in the way.

Once more, in a favorite corner of the big front porch, she was just beginning to find some comfort with her doll when the woman with the broom forced her to move again.

Poor little girl! What could she do under such trying circumstances--what indeed but go to mother. All the way up the long stairs she went to where mother was as busy as ever a mother could be doing something with a lot of things that were piled all over the room. But mother, when she saw the tear stained little face, understood in a flash and put aside whatever it was that she was doing, quickly, and held the little girl, dolly and all, close in her mother arms until the feeling of being in the way and of not being wanted was all gone. And, when the tears were quite dry, mother said, so gently that it did not hurt, "No dearie, I'm afraid you can't help mother now because mother's girl is too little to understand what it is that mother is doing. But I'll tell you something that you *can* do. Mother will give you some things from the pantry and you may go over to see the little boy. And I am as sure, as sure can be, that, when he sees all the nice things you have, he will play keeping house with you."

So the little girl in the Yesterdays, with her treasures from mother's pantry, went out across the garden and through the hedge to find the boy. Very carefully she went through the opening in the hedge so that she would lose none of her treasures. And oh, the joy of it! The splendid wonder of it! She found that the boy had built a house--all by himself he had built it--with real boards, and had furnished it with tiny chairs and tables made from boxes. Complete it was, even to a beautiful strip of carpet on the floor and a shelf on which to put the dishes. Then, indeed, when the boy told her how he had made the house for her--just for her--and how it was to have been a surprise; and that she had come just in time because if she tad come sooner it would have spoiled the fun--the heart of the little girl overflowed with gladness. And to think that all the time she was feeling so not wanted and in the way the boy was doing *this* and all for her! Did her mother know? She rather guessed that she did; mothers have such a marvelous way of knowing everything, particularly the nicest things.

So the little girl gave the boy all the treasures that she had brought so carefully and they had great fun eating them together; and all the rest of that day they played "keephouse." And this is why that day was among the best of all the woman's Yesterdays.

Several men going home from work passed the spot where the young woman sat. Then a group of shop girls followed; then another group and, in turn, two women from an office that did not close early on Saturdays. After them a young girl who looked very tired came walking alone, and then there were more men and women in a seemingly endless procession. And so many girls and women there were in the procession that the woman, as she came back from her Yesterdays, wondered who was left to make homes for the world.

The sun was falling now in long bars and shafts of light between the buildings and the trees, and the windows of the house where the man had been fixing the roof were blazing as if in flames. The man had taken down his ladder and gone away. It was time the young woman was going home. And as she went, joining the procession of laborers, her heart was filled with longing--with longing and with hope. The boy of her Yesterdays lived only in those days that were gone. He had no place in the dreams of her womanhood. He was only the playmate of the little girl. Even as those years were gone the boy had gone out of her life. But somewhere, perhaps, that one who was to go with her through the old, old, open door was even then building for her a home--their home. Perhaps, some day, an all wise Mother Nature would tell her to leave the world that gave her no welcome--that could not recognize her womanhood--that made her heart rebel in humiliation and shame--and go to do her woman's work.

Very carefully would she go when the time came, taking all the treasures of her womanhood. She would go very carefully that none of her treasures be lost.

KNOWLEDGE

THE green of the pastures and the gold of the fields was buried so deeply under banks of snow that no one could say: "Here the cattle fed and the buttercups grew; there the grain was harvested; here the corn stood in shocks; there the daisies and meadow grass sheltered the nest of the bo-bo-link." As death calls alike the least and the greatest back to the dust from which they came, so winter laid over the varied and changing scenes of summer a cold, white, shroud of wearisome sameness. The birds were hundreds of miles away in their sunny southland haunts. The bees, the butterflies, and many of the tiny wood folk, were all snugly tucked in their winter beds, dreaming, perhaps, as they slept, of the sunshiny summer days. In the garden the wind had heaped a great drift high against the hedge on the boy's side, and, on the little girl's side, the cherry tree in the corner stood shivering in its nakedness with bare arms uplifted as though praying for mercy to the stinging cold wind.

In the city the snow, as fast as it fell, was stained by soot and grime and lay in the streets a mass of filth. The breath of the laboring truck horses arose from their wide nostrils like clouds of steam and, in the icy air, covered their breasts and shoulders and sides with a coat of white frost. The newsboys and vendors of pencils and shoestrings shivered in nooks and corners and doorways and, as the people went with heads bent low before the freezing blast that swirled through the narrow canyons between the tall buildings, the snowy pavement squeaked loudly under their feet.

And the man who had found something to do, from his Occupation, began to acquire Knowledge. In doing things, he began to know things.

But the man had to gain first a knowledge of Knowledge. He first had to learn this: that a man might know all about a thing without ever knowing the thing itself. He had to understand that Knowledge is not knowing *about a thing but knowing the thing*. When first he had dreamed his manhood dreams, before he had found something to do, the man, quite modestly, thought that he knew a great deal. In his school days, he had exhausted many text books and had passed many creditable examinations upon many subjects and so he had thought that he knew a great deal. And he did. He knew a great deal *about* things. But when he had found something to do, and had tried to do it, he found also very quickly that, although he knew so much about the thing he had to do, he knew very, very, little of the thing itself and that only knowledge of the thing itself could ever help him to realize his dreams.

From his Occupation, he learned this also: that Knowledge is not what some other man knows and tells you but what the thing that you have found to do makes known to you. Knowledge is not told, *cannot* be told, to one by another, even though that other has it abundantly for, to the one to whom it is told, it remains ever what someone else knows. What the thing that a man finds to do makes known to him, *that* is Knowledge. So Knowledge is to be had not from books alone but rather from Life. So idleness is a vicious ignorance and those who do the most are wisest.

Before he had found something to do the man had called himself a thinker. But when he tried to do the thing that he had found to do, he quickly realized that he had only thought that he thought. He found that he was not at all a thinker but a listener--a receiver--a rememberer. In his school days, the thoughts of others were offered him and he, because he had accepted them, called them his own. He came, now, to understand that thinking is not accepting the thoughts of others but finding thoughts of your own in whatever it is that you have found to do.

Thinking the thoughts of others is a delightful pastime and profitable but it is not really thinking. Also, if one be blessed with a good memory, he may thus cheaply acquire a reputation for great wisdom; just as one, if he happens to be born with a nose of uncommon length or bigness, may attract the attention of the world. But no one should deceive himself. A man because he is able, better than the multitude, to repeat the thoughts of other men must not therefore think himself a better thinker than the crowd. No more should the one with the uncommon nose flatter himself that he is necessarily handsome or distinguished in appearance because the people notice him. He who attracts the attention of the world should inquire most carefully into the reason for the gathering of the crowd; for a crowd will gather as readily to listen to a mountebank as to hear an angel from heaven.

To repeat what others have thought is not at all evidence that he who remembers is thinking. Great thoughts are often repeated thoughtlessly. A man's Occupation betrays him or establishes his claim to Knowledge. That which a man does proclaims that which he thinks or in his thoughtlessness finds him out.

Of course, when the man had learned this, he said at first, quite wrongly, that his school days were wasted. He said that what he had called his education was all a mistake--that it was vanity only and wholly worthless. But, as he went on gaining ever more and more Knowledge from the thing that he was doing, and, through that thing, of many other things, he came to understand that his school days were not wasted but very well spent indeed. He came to see that what he had called education was not a mistake. He came to understand that what was wrong was this: he had considered his education complete, finished, when he had only been prepared to begin. He had considered his schooling as an end to be gained when it was only a means to the end. He had considered his learning as wealth to hold when it was capital to invest. He had mistaken the thoughts that he received from others for Knowledge when they were given him only to inspire and to help him in acquiring Knowledge.

And then, of this knowledge of Knowledge gained by the man from his Occupation, there was born in him a mighty passion, a burning desire. It was the passion for Knowledge. It was the desire to know. To know the thing that he had found to do was not enough. He determined to use that knowledge to gain Knowledge of many other things. He felt within himself a new strength stirring--the strength of thought. He saw that knowledge of things led ever to more knowledge, even as link to link in a golden chain. One end of the chain he held in his Occupation; the other was somewhere, far beyond his sight, hidden in the mists that shroud the Infinite Fact, fast to the mighty secret of Life itself. Link by link, he determined to follow the chain. From knowing things to knowledge of other things he would go even until he held in his grip the last link--until he held the key to the riddle--until he knew the answer to the sum of Life.

And facts--cold, uncompromising, all powerful, unanswerable facts--should give him this mastering knowledge of Life. For him there should be no sentiment to deceive, no illusion to beguile, no fancy to lead astray. As resistlessly as the winter, with snowflake upon snowflake, had buried all the delightful vagaries of summer, so this man, in his passion for Knowledge, would have buried all the charming inconsistencies, the beautiful inaccuracies, the lovely pretenses of Life. The illusions, the sentiment, the fancies, the poetry of Life, he would have buried under the icy sameness of his facts, even as the flowers and grasses were hidden under winter's shroud of snow. But he could not. Under the snow, summer still lived. Under the cold facts of Life, the tender sentiments, the fond fancies, the dear illusions have strength even as the flowers and grasses.

I do not know what it was that brought it about. It does not matter what it was. Perhaps it was the sight of some boys coasting down a little hill, on a side street, near where the man lived at this time: perhaps it was a group of children who, on their way home from school, were waging a merry snow fight: or, perhaps, it was the man's own effort to acquire Knowledge: or, it may be, that his brain was weary, that the way of Knowledge seemed over long, that the links in the golden chain were many and passed all too slowly through his hand--I do not know--but, whatever it was that did it, the man, as he sat before his fire that winter evening with a too solid and substantial book, slipped away from his grown up world of facts back into the no less real world of childhood, back into his Yesterdays--to a school day in his Yesterdays.

Once again he made his way in the morning to the little schoolhouse that stood half way up a long hill, in the edge of a bit of timber, nearly two miles from his home. The yard, beaten smooth and hard by many bare and childish feet, was separated from the timber by a rail fence but was left open in front to any stray horses or cattle that, wandering down the road, might be tempted to rest a while in the shade of a great tree that stood near the center of the little clearing. The stumps of the other forest beauties that had once, like this tree, tossed their branches in the sunlight were still holding the places that God had given them and made fine seats for the girls or bases for the boys when they played ball at recess or noon. And often, when the shouting youngsters had been called from their sports by the rapping of the teacher's ruler at the door and only the busy hum of their childish voices came floating through the open windows, a venturesome squirrel or a saucy chipmunk would creep stealthily along the fence, stopping now and then to sit bolt upright with tail in air to look and listen. Then suddenly, at sight of a laughing face at the window or the appearance of some boy who had gained the coveted permission to get a bucket of water, the little visitor would whisk away again like a flash and, with a warning chatter to his mate, would seek safety among the leaves and branches of the forest only to reappear once more when all was quiet until, at last, made bold by many trials, he would leap from the fence and scamper across the yard to take possession of the tallest stump as though he himself were a schoolboy. Sometimes a crow, after carefully watching the place for a little while from a safe position on the fence across the road, would fly quietly down to look for choice bits dropped from the dinner baskets of the children. Or again, a long, lazy, black snake would crawl across the yard to search for the little mice that lived in the foundation of the house and in the corners of the fence. Or, perhaps, a chicken hawk, that had been sailing on outstretched wings in ever narrowing circles, would drop from the blue sky to claim his share of the plunder only to be frightened away again by the sound of the teacher's voice raised in sharp rebuke of some mischievous urchin.

The schoolhouse was not a large building nor was it, in the least, imposing. It was built of wood with a foundation of rough stone and there were heavy shutters which were always carefully closed at night to keep out the tramps who might seek a lodging place within. And there was a woodshed, too, where the boys romped upon rainy days and where was fought many a schoolboy battle for youthful love and honor. The building had once been painted white but the storm and sunshine of many months had worn away the paint, and there remained only the dark, weather stained, boards save beneath the cornice and the window ledge where one might still find traces of its former glory. The chimney, too, was old and some of the bricks had crumbled and fallen from the top which made it look ragged against the sky. And the steps and threshold were worn very thin--very, very, thin.

Wearied with his passion for Knowledge; tired of his cold facts; hungering in his heart for a bit of wholesome sentiment as one in winter hungers for the summer flowers; the man who sat before his fire that night, with a too heavy and substantial book, crossed once more with childish feet the worn threshold of the old schoolhouse and stood within the entry where hung the hats and dinner baskets of his mates. They looked very familiar to him--those hats--and, as he saw them in his memory, each offered mute testimony to its owner's disposition and rank in childhood's world. There were broad brimmed straws that belonged to the patient, plodding, boys and caps that seemed made to set far back on the heads of the boisterous lads. There was the old slouch felt of the poor boy who did chores for his board and the brimless hat of the bully of the school. There were the trim sailors of the good little boys and the head gear of his own particular chum. And there--the man who sought Knowledge only in facts smiled at the fire and a fond light came into his eyes while his too solid and substantial hook slipped unheeded to the floor--there was a sunbonnet of blue checkered gingham hanging by its long strings from a hook near the window.

With fast beating heart, the boy saw that the next hook was vacant and placing his own well worn straw beside the bonnet he wondered if she would know whose hat it was. And then once more, with reluctant hand, the seeker of Knowledge, in his Yesterdays, pushed open the door leading to the one room in the building and, with a sigh of regret, passed from the bright sunlight of boyish freedom to the shadow of his childish task.

There were neither tinted walls nor polished woodwork in that hall of learning. But, thank God, learning does not depend upon tinted walls or polished woodwork. Indeed it seems that rude rafters and unplastered ceilings most often covers the head of learning. The humble cottage of the farmer shelters many a true scholar and statesmen are bred in log cabins. Neither was there a furnace with mysterious cranks and chains nor steam pipes nor radiators. But, when the cold weather came, the room was warmed by an old sheet iron stove that stood near the center of the building with an armful of wood in a box nearby and the kindlings for to-morrow's fire drying on the floor beneath. The desks were of soft pine, without paint or varnish, but carved with many a quaint and curious figure by jack knives in the hands of ambitious youngsters. The seats were rude benches worn smooth and shiny. A water bucket had its place near the door and a rusty tin dipper that leaked quite badly hung from a nail in the casing.

And hanging upon the dingy wall were the old maps and charts that, torn and soiled by long usage, had patiently guided generations of boys and girls through the mysteries of lands and seas, icebergs, trade winds, deserts, and plains. Still patiently they marked for the boy's bewildered brain latitude and longitude, the tropic of cancer, the arctic circle, and the poles. Were they hanging there still? the man wondered. Were they still patiently leading the way through a wilderness of islands and peninsulas, capes and continents, rivers, lakes, and sounds? Or had they, in the years that had gone since he looked upon their learned faces, been sunk to oblivion in the depths of their own oceans by the weight of their own mountain ranges? And, suddenly, the man who sought Knowledge in facts found himself wishing in his heart that some gracious being would make for older children maps and charts that they might know where flow the rivers of prosperity, where rise the mountains of fame, where ripple the lakes of love, where sleep the valleys of rest, or where thunders the ocean of truth.

At one end of the old schoolroom, behind the teacher's desk, was a blackboard with its accompanying chalk, erasers, rulers, and bits of string. To the boy, that blackboard was a trial, a temptation, a vindication, or a betrayal. Often, as he sat with his class on the long recitation seat that faced the teacher's desk, with half studied lesson, but with bright hopes of passing the twenty minutes safely, before the slow hand of the old clock had marked but half the time, his hopes would be blasted by a call to the board where he would bring upon himself the ridicule of his schoolmates, the condemnation of the teacher, and would take his seat to hear, with burning cheeks, the awful sentence: "You may study your lesson after school."

After school--sorrowfully the boy saw the others passing from the room, leaving him behind. And the last to go, glancing back with tear dimmed eyes, was the little girl. Sadly he listened to the voices in the entry and heard their shouts as they burst out doors; and--suddenly, his heart beat quicker and his cheeks burned--*that* was her voice!

Clear and sweet through the open window of the man's memory it came--the voice of his little girl mate of the Yesterdays.

She was standing on the worn threshold of the old schoolhouse, calling to her friends to wait; and the boy knew that she was lingering there for him and that she called to her companions loudly so that he would understand.

But the teacher knew it too and bade the little girl go home.

Then, while the boy listened to that sweet voice growing fainter and fainter in the distance; while he saw her, in his fancy, walking slowly, lagging behind her companions, looking back for him; the teacher talked to him very seriously about the value of his opportunities; told him that to acquire an education was his duty; sought to impress upon him that the most important thing in life was Knowledge.

Of course, thought the boy, teacher must know. And, thinking this, he felt himself to be a very bad boy, indeed; because, in his heart, he knew that he would have, that moment, given up every chance of an education; he would have sacrificed every hope of wisdom; he would have thrown away all Knowledge and heaven itself just to be walking down the road with the little girl. And he must have been a little bad--that boy--because also, most ardently, did he wish that he was big enough to thrash the teacher or whoever it was that invented blackboards.

As the man stooped to take up again his too solid and substantial book, he felt that he was but a schoolboy still. To him, the world had become but a great blackboard. In his private life or in conversation with a friend, he might hide his poorly prepared lesson behind a show of fine talk, a pet quotation, or an air of learning; but when he was forced to put what he knew where all men might see--when he was made to write his sentences in books or papers or compelled to do his problems in the business world--then it was that his lack of preparation was discovered, and that he brought upon himself the ridicule or condemnation of his fellows. Unconsciously he listened, half expecting to hear again the old familiar sentence: "You may study your lesson after school." After school--would there be any after school, he wondered.

"And, after all, was that teacher in his Yesterdays right?" the man asked himself. "Was Knowledge the most important thing in life? After all, was that schoolboy of the Yesterdays such a bad schoolboy because, in his boyish heart, he rebelled against the tasks that kept him from his schoolmates and from the companionship of the little girl? Was that boy so bad because he wished that he was big enough to thrash whoever it was that invented blackboards, to rob schoolboys of their schoolgirl mates?"

Suppose--the man asked himself, as he laid aside the too heavy and substantial book and looked into the fire again--suppose, that, after a lifetime devoted to the pursuit of Knowledge, there should be no one, when school time was over, to linger on the worn old threshold for him? Suppose he should be forced, in the late afternoon, to go down the homeward road alone? Could it be truly said that his manhood years had been well spent? Could any number of accumulated facts satisfy him if the hour was a lonely hour when school closed for the day? Might it not be that there is a Knowledge to be gained from Life that is of more value than the wintry Knowledge of facts?

As the man looked back into his Yesterdays, the blackboard and its condemnation mattered little to him. It was the going home alone that mattered. What, he wondered, would matter most when, at last, he could look back upon his grown up school days--the world blackboard with its approval or its condemnation, or the going home alone?

* * * * *

It was the time of melting snow. The top of the orchard hill was a faded brown patch as though, on a shoulder of winter's coat, the season had worn a hole quite through; while the fields of the fall plowing made spots that looked pitifully thin and threadbare; and the creek, below the house where the little girl lived, was a long dark line looking for all the world like a rip where the icy stitching of a seam in the once proud garment had, at last, given way. But the drift in the garden on the boy's side of the hedge was still piled high against the barrier of thickly interwoven branches and twigs and the cherry tree, in its shivering nakedness, seemed to be pleading, now, for spring to come quickly.

The woman who knew herself to be a woman did not attempt to walk home from her work that Saturday afternoon. The streets were too muddy and she was later than usual because of some extra work.

Of her Occupation--of the world into which she had gone--the woman also was gaining Knowledge. Though, she did not learn from choice but because she must. And she learned of her work only what was needful for her to know that she might hold her place. She had no desire to know more. Because the woman already knew the supreme thing, she had no desire to learn more of her Occupation than she must. Already she knew her womanhood, and that, to a woman who knows, is the supreme thing. For a woman with understanding there is no Knowledge greater than this: the knowledge of her womanhood. There was born in her no passion for knowledge of things. She burned with no desire to follow the golden chain, link by link, to its hidden end. In her womanhood she held already the answer to the sum of Life.

The passion of her womanhood was not to *know but to trust*--not *facts but faith*--not *evidence but belief*--not *reason but emotion*. Her desire was not to take from the world by the power of Knowledge but to receive from the world by right of her sex and love. She did not crave the independence of great learning but longed, rather, for the prouder dependence of a true womanhood. Out of her woman heart's fullness she pitied and fed the poor mendicant without inquiring into the economic condition that made him a beggar. Her situation, she accepted with secret rebellion, with hidden shame and humiliation in her heart, but never asked why the age forced her into such a position. For affection, for sympathy, for confidence, and understanding, she hungered with a woman hunger; and, through her hunger for these, from the men and women with whom she labored she gained Knowledge of Life. Of the lives of her fellow workers--of the women who had entered that world, even as she had entered it, because they must--of the men whom she came to know under circumstances that forbade recognition of her womanhood--she gained Knowledge; and the Knowledge she gained was this: that the world is a world of hungry hearts.

I do not know just what the circumstances were under which the woman learned this. I do not know what her Occupation was nor who her friends were; nor can I tell in detail of the peculiar incidents that led to this Knowledge. Such things are not of my story. This, only, belongs to my story: the woman learned that the world is a world of hungry hearts. Cold and cruel and calculating and bold, fighting desperately, merciless, and menacing, the world is but a hungry hearted world with it all. This, when a woman knows it, is, for her, a saving Knowledge. Just to the degree that a woman knows this, she is wise above all men--wise with a wisdom that men cannot attain. Just to the degree that a woman is ignorant of this, she is unlearned in the world's best wisdom.

Long before she knocked at the door of the world into which she had been admitted, upon condition that she left her womanhood without, the woman had thought herself wise in knowledge of mankind. In her school days, text books and lessons had meant little to her beside the friendship of her schoolmates. At her graduation she had considered her life education complete. She thought, modestly, that she was fitted for a woman's place in life. And that which she learned first from the world into which she had gone was this: that her knowledge of life was very, very, meager; that there were many, many, things about men and women that she did not know.

School could fit her only for the fancy work of Life: plain sewing she must learn of Life itself. School had made her highly ornamental: Life must make her useful. School had developed her capacity for pleasure and enjoyment: not until Life had developed her capacity for sorrow and pain would her education be complete. School had taught her to speak, to dress, and to act correctly: Life must teach her to feel. School had trained her mind to appreciate: Life must teach her to sympathize. School had made her a lady: Life must make the lady a woman.

The woman had known her life schoolmates only in pleasure--in those hours when they came to her seeking to please or desiring to be pleased. In her Occupation she was coming to know them in their hours of toil, when there was no thought of gaining or giving pleasure, but only of the demands of their existence; when duty, pitiless, stern, uncompromising, duty held them in its grip; when need, unrelenting, ever present, dominating need, drove them under its lash. She had known them only in their hours of leisure--when their minds were free for the merry jest, the ready laugh, the quick sympathy: now she was coming to know them in those other hours when their minds were intent upon the battle they waged--when their thoughts were all of the attack, the defense, the advance, the retreat, the victory or defeat. She had known them only in their hours of rest--when their hands were empty, their nerves and muscles relaxed, their hearts calm and their brains cool; now she saw them when their hands held the weapons of their warfare--the tools of their craft--when their nerves and muscles were braced for the strain of the conflict or tense with the effort of toil; when their hearts beat high with the zeal of their purpose and their brains were fired with the excitement of their efforts. She had known them only in the hours of their dreaming--when, as they looked out upon life, they talked confidently of the future: she was learning now to know them when they were working out their dreams; at times with hopes high and courage strong; at other times discouraged, frightened, and dismayed. She had known them only as they dreamed of the past--when they talked in low tones of the days that were gone: now she saw them as they thought only of the present and the days that were to come. So this woman, from the world into which she had gone, gained knowledge of mankind.

And this is the pity and the danger of it: that the woman gained this knowledge from a world, that, even as it taught her, denied her womanhood. The sadness of it all is this: to the world that refused to recognize her womanhood, it was given to teach her that which would make her womanhood complete. The knowledge that she must have to complete her womanhood the woman should have gained only from the life of her dreams--the life that is beyond that old, old, open door through which she could not pass alone. In the companionship, sympathy, strength, protection, and love, of that one who was to cross with her the threshold of the door that God set open in the beginning, she should have gained the knowledge of life that would ripen her girlhood into womanhood. For what else, indeed, has God given love to men and women? In the strength that would come to her with her children, the woman should have been privileged to learn sorrow and pain. In the world that would have honored, above all else, her womanhood, she should have been permitted to find the knowledge of life that would perfect and complete her womanhood.

Fruit, I know, may be picked green from the tree and artificially forced to a kind of ripeness. But the fruit that matures under Nature's careful hand; that knows in its ripening the warm sunshine and the cleansing showers, the cool of the quiet evening and the freshness of the dewy morn, the strength of the roaring storms and the softness of the caressing breeze--this fruit alone, I say, has the flavor that is from heaven.

It is a trite saying that many a girl of sixteen, these days, knows more of life than her grandmother knew at sixty. It remains to be proven that, because of this knowledge, the young woman of today is a better woman than her grandmother was. But, as the only positive proof would be her children, the case is very likely to be thrown out of court for lack of evidence for it seems, somehow, that, when women gain Knowledge from that world into which they go alone, leaving their womanhood behind, they acquire also a strange pride in being too wise to mate for love or to bear children. And yet, it is true, that the knowledge that enables a woman to live happy and contented without children is a damnable knowledge and a menace to the race.

Poor old world, you are so "grown up" these days and your palate is so educated to the artificial flavor that you have forgotten, seemingly, how peaches taste when ripened on the trees. God pity you, old world, if you do not soon get back into the orchard before you lose your taste for fruit altogether.

The knowledge that the woman gained from her Occupation made her question, more and more, if that one with whom she could cross the threshold of the door that led to the life of her dreams, would ever come. The knowledge she gained made her doubt her courage to enter that door with him if he should come. In the knowledge she gained of the world into which she had gone alone, her womanhood's only salvation was this: that she gained also the knowledge that the world of men, even as the world of women, is a world of hungry hearts. It was this that kept her--that made her strong--that saved her. It was this knowledge that saved her womanhood for herself and for the race.

The week, for the woman, had been a hard week. The day, for her, had been a hard day. When she boarded the car to go to her home she was very tired and she was not quite the picture of perfect woman health that she had been that other Saturday--the time of falling leaves.

For some unaccountable reason there was one vacant seat left in the car and she dropped into it with a little inward sigh of relief. With weary, unseeing, eyes she stared out of the window at the throng of people hurrying along through the mud and slush of the streets. Her tired brain refused to think. Her very soul was faint with loneliness and the knowledge that she was gaining of life.

The car stopped again and a party of girls of the high school age, evidently just from the Saturday matinee, crowded in. Clinging to the straps and the backs of seats, clutching each other with little gusts and ripples of laughter, they filled the aisle of the crowded car with a fresh and joyous life that touched the tired woman like a breath of spring. In all this work stale, stupidly weary, world there is nothing so refreshing as the wholesome laugh of a happy, care free, young girl. The woman whose heart was heavy with knowledge of life would have liked to take them in her arms. She felt a sense of gratitude as though she were indebted to them just for their being. And would these, too--the woman thought--would these, too, be forced by the custom of the age--by necessity--to go into the world that would not recognize their womanhood--that would put a price upon the priceless things of their womanhood--that would teach them hard lessons of life and, with a too early knowledge, crush out the sweet girlish naturalness, even as a thoughtless foot crushes a tender flower while still it is in the bud?

And thinking thus, perhaps because of her weariness, perhaps because of some chance word dropped by the girls as they talked of their school and schoolmates, the woman went back again into her Yesterdays--to the schoolmates of her Yesterdays. The world in which she now lived and labored was forgotten. Forgotten were the worries and troubles of her grown up life--forgotten the trials and disappointments--forgotten the new friends, the uncongenial acquaintances, the cruel knowledge, the heartless business--forgotten everything of the present--all, all, was lost in a golden mist of the long ago.

The tall, graceful, girl holding to a strap at the forward end of the car, in the woman's Yesterdays, lived just beyond the white church at the corner. The dark haired, dark eyed, round faced one, she knew as the minister's daughter. While the dainty, doll like, miss clinging to her sturdier sister, in those days of long ago, was the woman's own particular chum. And the girl with the yellow curls--the one with the golden hair--the blue eyed, and the brown--the slender and the stout--every one--belonged to the tired woman's Yesterdays--every one she had known in the past and to each she gave a name.

And then--as the woman, watching the young schoolgirls in the crowded car, lived once again those days of the old schoolhouse on the hill where, with her girl companions of the long ago, she sought the beginnings of Knowledge--the boys came, too. Just as in the Yesterdays they had come to take their places in the old schoolroom, they came, now, to take their places in the woman's memory.

There was the tall, thin, lad whose shoulders seemed, even in his school days, to find the burden of life too heavy; and who wore always on his face such a sad and solemn air that one was almost startled when he laughed as though the parson had cracked a joke at a funeral. The woman smiled as she remembered how his clothes were never known to fit him. When his trousers were so short that they barely reached below his knees his coat sleeves covered his hands and the skirts of that garment almost swept the ground; but, when the trousers were rolled up at the bottom and hung over his feet like huge bags, his long, thin, arms showed, half way to his elbows, in a coat that was too small to button about even his narrow chest. That boy never missed his lessons, though, but when he learned them no one ever knew for he seemed to be always drawing grotesque figures and funny faces on his slate or whittling slyly on some curious toy when the teacher's back was turned. He had no particular chum or crony. He was never a leader but dared to follow the boldest. To the little boys and girls he was a hero; to the older ones he was--"Slim."

The woman, by chance, had met this old schoolmate, one day, in her grown up world. In the editorial rooms of a large city daily he was the chief, and she noticed that his clothing fitted him a little better; that he was a little broader in the shoulders; a little larger around the waist; his face was not quite so solemn and his eyes had a more knowing look perhaps. But still--still--the woman could see that he was, after all, the same old "Slim" and she fancied, with another smile, that he often, still, whittled toys when the teacher's back was turned.

Then came the fat boy--"Stuffy." He, too, had another name which does not matter. Always in the Yesterdays, as in the to-days, there is a "Stuffy." "Stuffy" was evidently built to roll through life, pushed gently by that special providence that seems to look after the affairs of fat people. His teeth were white and even, his eyes of the deepest blue, and his nose--what there was of it--was almost hidden by cheeks that were as red and shiny as the apples he always carried in his pocket. He was very generous with those same apples--was "Stuffy"--though one was tempted to think that he shared his fruit not so much from choice but rather because he disliked the hard work that was sure to follow a refusal of the pressing invitation to "go halvers." The woman fancied that she could see again the look of mingled fun and fear, generosity and greed, that went over her schoolmate's face as he saw the half of his eatable possessions pass into the keeping of his companions. And then, as he watched the tempting morsels disappear, the expression on his face would seem to show a battle royal between his stomach and his heart, in that he rejoiced to see the happiness of his friends, even while he coveted that which gave them pleasure. She wondered where was "Stuffy" now? She felt sure that he must live in a big house, and drive to and from his place of business in a fine carriage, with fine horses and a coachman in livery, and dine and wine his friends as often as he chose with never a fear that he would run short of good things for himself. She was quite sure, too, that he would suffer with severe attacks of gout at times and would have four or five half grown daughters and a wife of great ambition. Does he, she wondered, does he ever--in the whirl and rush of business or in the excitement and pleasure of his social life--does he ever go back to those other days? Does the grown up "Stuffy" remember how once he traded marbles for candy or bought sweet cakes with toys?

And then, there was the boy with the freckled face and tangled hair, whose nose seemed always trying to peep into his own mischief lighted eyes as though wishing to see what new deviltry was breeding there: and his crony, who never could learn the multiplication table, who was forever swearing vengeance on the teacher, whose clothes were always torn, and who carried frogs and little snakes in his pockets: and the timid boys who always played in one corner of the yard by themselves or with the girls or stood by and watched, with mingled admiration and envy, the games and pranks of the bolder lads: and "Dummy"--poor "Dummy"--the shining mark for every schoolboy trick and joke; with his shock of yellow hair, his weak cross eyes, his sharp nose, thin lips, and shambling, shuffling, shifting manner--poor "Dummy."

And of course there was a bully, the Ishmael of the school, whom everybody shunned and nobody liked; who fought the teacher and frightened the little children; who chewed, and smoked, and swore, and lied, and did everything bad that a boy could do. He had a few followers, a very few, who joined him rather through fear than admiration and not one of whom cared for or trusted him. The woman remembered how this schoolboy face was sadly hard and cold and cruel, as though, because he had gotten so little sunshine from life, his heart was frozen over. She had read of him, in the grown up world, receiving sentence for a dreadful crime, and, remembering his father and mother, had wondered if his grandparents were like them and how many generations before his birth his career of crime began.

Again and again, the car had stopped to let people off but the woman had not noticed. The schoolgirls, all but the tall one who had found a seat, were gone. But the woman had not seen them go.

And then, as she sat dreaming of the days long gone--as she saw again the faces of her school day friends, one there was that stood out from among them all. It was the face of the boy who lived next door--the boy who had stood with her under the cherry tree; who had put a tiny play ring of brass upon her finger; and who had kissed her with a kiss that was somehow different. He was the hero of her Yesterdays as he was the acknowledged chieftain of the school. No one could run so fast, swim so far, dive so deep, or climb so high as he. No one could throw him in wrestling or defeat him in boxing. He was their lord, their leader, their boyish master and royally he ruled them all--his willing subjects. He it was who stopped the runaway horse; who killed the big snake; and who pulled the minister's little daughter from the pond. It was he who planned the parties and the picnics; the sleigh rides in winter and the berrying trips in summer. It was he whom the girls all loved and the boys all worshiped--bold, handsome, daring, dashing, careless, generous, leader of the Yesterdays.

Again she saw his face lifted slyly from a spelling book to smile at her across the aisle. Again she felt the rich, warm, color rush to her cheeks as he took his seat, beside her on the recitation bench. Again her eyes were dimmed with tears when he was punished for some broken rule or shone with gladness when she heard his clear voice laughing with his friends or calling to his mates and her.

And once again, in the late afternoon, with him and with the other boys and girls, she went down the road from the little schoolhouse in the edge of the timber on the hill; her sunbonnet hanging by its strings and her dinner basket on her arm. Onward, through the long shadows that lay across their way, they went together, to pause at last before the gate of her home, there to linger for a little, while the others still went on. Farther and farther in the evening they watched their schoolmates go--up the road past the house where he lived--past the orchard and over the hill--until, in the distance, they seemed to vanish into the sunset sky and she was left with him alone.

The conductor called the woman's street but she did not heed. The man in uniform pulled the bell cord and, as the car stopped, called again, looking toward her expectantly. But she did not notice. With a smile, the man, who knew her, approached, and: "Beg your pardon Miss, but here's your street."

With blushing cheeks and confused manner, she stammered her thanks, and hurried from the car amid the smiles of the passengers. And the woman did not know how beautiful she was at that moment. She was wondering: in the hungry hearted world--

under all his ambition, plans, and labor, with the knowledge that must have come to him also from life--was his heart ever hungry too?

IGNORANCE

WHEN the man had gained a little knowledge from the thing that he had found to do and had wearied himself greatly trying to follow the golden chain, link by link, to the very end, he came, then, to understand the value of Ignorance. He came to see that success in working out his dreams depended quite as much upon Ignorance as upon Knowledge--that, indeed, to know the value of Ignorance is the highest order of Knowledge.

There are a great many things about this man's life that I do not know. But that does not matter because most of the things about any man's life are of little or no importance. That the man came to know the value of Ignorance was a thing of vast importance to the man and, therefore, is of importance to my story. Ignorance also is one of the Thirteen Truly Great Things of Life but only those who have much knowledge know its value.

A wise Ignorance is rich soil from which the seeds of Knowledge will bring forth fruit, a hundred fold. "I do not know": this is the beginning and the end of wisdom. One who has never learned to say: "I do not know," has not the A B C of education. He who professes to be educated but will not confess Ignorance is intellectually condemned.

A man who pretends to a knowledge which he has not is like a pygmy wearing giant's clothing, ridiculous: but he who admits Ignorance is like a strong knight, clothed in a well fitting suit of mail, ready to achieve truth.

When a man declares openly his ignorance concerning things of which he knows but little, the world listens with increased respect when he speaks of the thing he knows: but when a man claims knowledge of all things, the world doubts mightily that he knows much of anything, and accepts questioningly whatever he says of everything.

That which a man does not know harms him not at all, neither does it harm the world; but that which, through a shallow, foolish, self-conceit, he professes to know, when he has at best only a half knowledge, or, in a self destructive vanity, deceives himself into thinking that he knows, betrays him always to the injury of both himself and others. An honest Ignorance is a golden vessel, empty, ready to be filled with wealth but a pretentious or arrogant knowledge is a vessel so filled with worthless trash that there is no room for that which is of value.

The world is as full of things to know as it is full of hooks, No man can hope to read all the books in the world. Selection is enforced by necessity. So it is in Knowledge. One should not think that, because a man is ignorant of some things, he is therefore a fool; his ignorance may be the manifestation of a choice wiser than that of the one who elects to sit in judgment upon him.

With the passion to know fully aroused; with his mind fretting to grapple with the problem of Life; and his purpose fired to solve the riddle of time; the man succeeded in acquiring this: that he must dare to know little. He came to understand that, while all knowable things are for all mankind to know, no man can know them all; and that the wisest men to whom the world pays highest tribute, are the wisest because they have not attempted to know all, but, recognizing the value of Ignorance, have dared to remain ignorant of much. Intellectual giants they are; intellectual babes they are, also. The man had thought that there was nothing that these men--these wise ones--did not know. He came to understand that even *he* knew some things of which they were ignorant. So his determination to know all things passed to a determination to know nothing of many things that he might know more of the things that were most closely associated with his life and work. He determined to know the most of the things that, to him, were most vital.

He saw also that he must work out his dreams within the circle of his own limitations; and that his limitations were not the limitations of his fellow workers; neither were their limitations his. He did not know yet just where the outmost circle of his limitations lay but he knew that it was there and that he must make no mistake when he came to it. And this, too, is true: just to the degree that the man recognized his limitations, the circle widened.

Also the man came to understand that there are things knowable and things unknowable. He came to see that truest wisdom is in this: for one to spend well his strength on the knowable things and refuse to dissipate his intellectual vigor upon the unknowable. Not until he began really to know things was he conscious in any saving degree of the unknowable. He saw that those who strive always with the unknowable beat the air in vain and exhaust themselves in their senseless folly. He saw that to concern oneself wholly with the unknowable is to rob the world of the things in which are its life. To meditate much upon the unknowable is an intellectual dissipation that produces spiritual intoxication and often results in spiritual delirium tremens. A habitual spiritual drunkard is a nuisance in the world. The wisdom of Ignorance is in nothing more apparent than in a clear recognition of the unknowable.

And then the man came to regret knowing some of the things that he knew. He came, in some things, to wish with all his heart that he had Ignorance where he had Knowledge. He found that much of the time and strength that he desired to spend in acquiring the knowledge that would help him to work out his dreams, he must spend, instead, in ridding himself of knowledge that he had already acquired. He learned that to forget is quite as necessary as to remember and very often much more difficult. Young he was, and strong he was, but, already, he felt the dragging power of the things he would have been better for not knowing--the things he desired to forget. They were very little things in comparison to the things that in the future he would wish to forget; but to him, at this time, they did not seem small. So it was that, in his effort to acquire Knowledge, the man began to strive also for Ignorance.

I do not know what it was that the man had learned that he desired to forget. My story is not the kind of a story that tells those things. I know, only, that for him to forget was imperative. I know, only, that had he held fast to Ignorance in some things of which he had gained knowledge, it would have been better. For him in some things Ignorance would have been the truest wisdom. Ignorance would have helped him to work out his dreams when Knowledge only hindered by forcing him to spend much time striving to forget. Those who know too much of evil find it extremely difficult to gain knowledge of the good. Those who know too much of the false find it very hard to recognize the true. A too great knowledge of things that are wrong makes it almost impossible for one to believe in that which is right. Ignorance, rightly understood, is, indeed, one of the Thirteen Truly Great Things of Life.

And then this man, in learning the value of Ignorance, came perilously near believing that no man could *know* anything. He came dangerously near the belief that Knowledge is all a mirage toward which men journey hopelessly; a phantom to be grasped by no hand; a will-o'-the-wisp to be followed here and there but leading nowhere. He, for a little, said that Ignorance is the truest wisdom. He believed, for a time, that to say always: "I do not know," is the height of all intelligence. One by one, he saw his intellectual idols fall in the dust of the commonplace. Little by little, he discovered that the intellectual masters he had served were themselves only servants. His intellectual Gods, he found to be men like himself. And so, for a while, he said: "We can know nothing. We can only think that we know. We can only pretend to know. There *is* no real Knowledge but only Ignorance. Ignorance should be exalted. In Ignorance lies peace, contentment, happiness, and safety." Even of his work--of his dreams he said this. He said: "It is no use." To the very edge of this pit he came but he did not fall in.

To accept the fact of the unknowable without losing his faith in the knowable: to recognize the unknown without losing in the least his grip upon the known: to find the Knowledge of Yesterday becoming the Ignorance of to-day and still hold fast to the Knowledge of the present; to watch his intellectual leaders dropping to the rear and to follow as bravely those who were still in the front: to see his intellectual heroes fall and his intellectual idols crumbling in the dust and still to keep burning the fire of his enthusiasm: to find Knowledge so often a curse and Ignorance a blessing and still to desire Knowledge: all this, the man learned that he must do if he would work out his dreams. That which saved the man from the pit of hopeless disbelief in everything and helped him to a clear understanding of Ignorance, was this: he went back again into his Yesterdays.

From sheltered fence corners and hidden woodland hollows, from the lee of high banks, and along the hedge in the garden, the last worn and ragged remnant of winter's garment was gone. The brook in the valley, below the little girl's house, had broken the last of its fetters and was rejoicing boisterously in its freedom. The meadow and pasture lands showed the tender green of the first grass life. Pussy willow buds were swelling and over the orchard and the wood a filmy veil of summer color was dropped as though by fairy hands. In the cherry tree, a pair of brown birds, just returning from their southern home, were discussing the merits of the nearby hedge as a building site: the madam bird insisting, as women will, that the beautiful traditions of the spot made it, for home building, peculiarly desirable. It was a well known fact, said she, that brown birds had builded there for no one knows how many ages. Even in the far away city, the man felt the season in the air. The reek of city odors could not altogether drown the subtle perfume that betrayed the near presence of the spring. As though the magic of the budding, sprouting, starting, time of the year placed him under its spell, the man went back to the springtime of his life--back into his Yesterdays.

Once again, he walked under the clear skies of childhood. Once again, he lived in the blessed, blessed, days when he had nothing to forget--when his mind and life were as a mountain brook that, clear and pure, from the spring of its birth runs ever onward, outward, turning never back, pausing never to form stagnant, poisonous, pools. And there it was--in his Yesterdays--in the pure sunlight of childhood--that he found new intellectual faith--that he came to a right understanding of the real wisdom of Ignorance.

The intellectual giants of his Yesterdays--those wise ones upon whose learning he looked with childish awe--who were they? Famous scholars who lectured in caps and gowns and words of many syllables upon themes of mighty interest to themselves? Students who, in their laboratory worlds, discovered many wonderful things that were not so and solved many puzzling problems with solutions that were right and entirely satisfactory until the next graduating class discovered them to be all wrong and no solution at all? Great religious leaders who were supernaturally called, divinely commissioned, and armed with holy authority to point out the true and only way of life until some other with the same call, commission, and authority, pointed out a wholly different true and only way? Great statesmen upon whose knowledge and leadership the salvation of the nation depended, until the next election discovered them to be foolish puppets of a dishonest and corrupt party and put new leaders in their places to save the nation with a new brand of political salvation, the chief value of which was its newness? No indeed! Such as these were not the intellectual giants of the man's Yesterdays. The heights of knowledge in those days were held by others than these.

One of the very highest peaks in the whole mountain range of learning, in the Yesterdays, was held by the hired man. Again, at chore time, the boy followed this wise one about the stables and the barn, watching, from a safe position near the door, while the horses were groomed and bedded down for the night. Again the pungent odors from the stalls, the scent of the straw and the hay in the loft, the smell of harness leather damp with sweat was in his nostrils and in his ears, the soft swish of switching tails, the thud of stamping hoofs, the contented munching of grain, the rustle of hay, with now and then a low whinny or an angry squeal. And fearlessly to and fro in this strange world moved the hired man. In and out among the horses he passed, perfectly at home in the stalls, seeming to share the most intimate secrets of the horse life.

Everything that there was to know about a horse, confidently thought the little boy, this wonderful man knew. The very language that he used when talking about horses was a language full of strange, hard, words, the meaning of which was hidden from the childish worshiper of wisdom. Such words as "ringbone" and "spavin" and "heaves" and "stringhalt" and "pastern" and "stifle" and "wethers" and "girth" and "hock," to the boy, seemed to establish, beyond all question, the intellectual greatness of the one who used them just as words of many syllables sometimes fix for older children the position on the intellectual heights of those who use them. "Chiaroscuro," "cheiropterous," "eschatology," and the "unearned increment"--who, in the common, every day, grown up, world, would dare question the artistic, scientific, religious, or political, knowledge of one who could talk like that?

Nor did the intellectual strength of this wise one of the Yesterdays exhaust itself with the scientific knowledge of horses. He was equally at home in the co-ordinate sciences of cows and pigs and chickens. Again the boy stood in the cow shed laboratory and watched, with childish wonder, the demonstration of the master's superior wisdom as the white streams poured into the tinkling milk pail. How did he do it--wondered the boy--where did this wizard in overalls and hickory shirt and tattered straw hat acquire his marvelous scientific skill?

In the garden, the orchard, or the field, it was the same. No secret of nature was hidden from this learned one. He knew whether potatoes should be planted in the dark or light of the moon: whether next winter would be "close" or "open": whether the coming season would be "early" or "late": whether next summer would be "wet" or "dry." Always he could tell, days ahead, whether it would rain or if the weather would be fair. With a peach tree twig he could tell where to dig for water. By many signs he could say whether luck would be good or bad. Small wonder that the boy felt very ignorant, very humble, in the presence of this wise one!

Then, one day, the boy, to his amazement, learned that this wizard of the barnyard knew nothing at all about fairies. Common, every day, knowledge was this knowledge of fairies to the boy: but the wise one knew nothing about them. So dense was his ignorance that he even seemed to doubt and smiled an incredulous smile when the boy tried to enlighten him.

It was a great day in his Yesterdays when the boy discovered that the hired man did not know about fairies.

As the years passed and the time approached when the boy was to become a man, he learned the meaning of many words that were as strange to the intellectual hero of his childhood as the language of that companion of horses had once been strange to him. In time, much of the knowledge of that barnyard sage became, to the boy, even as the boy's knowledge of fairies had been to the man. Still--still--it was a great day in his Yesterdays when the boy discovered that the hired man did not know about fairies. Perhaps, though, it was just as well that the hired man did not know. If he had become too familiar with the fairies, his potatoes might not have been planted either in the light or the dark of the moon and the world's potatoes must be planted somehow.

Equally great in his special field of knowledge was the old, white haired, negro who lived in a tiny cabin just a little way over the hill. Strange and awful were the things that *he* knew about the fearsome, supernatural, creatures, that lived and moved in the unseen world. Of "hants" and "spirits" and "witches" and "hoodoos" he told the boy with such earnest confidence and so convincing a manner that to doubt was impossible. In the unknowable world, the old negro moved with authority unquestioned, with piety above criticism, with a religious zeal of such warmth that the boy was often moved by the old man's wisdom and goodness to go to him with offerings from mother's pantry.

And then, one day, the boy discovered that this wonderfully wise one could neither read nor write. Everybody that the boy knew, in the grown up world, could read and write. The boy himself could even read "cat" and "rat" and "dog." Vaguely the boy wondered, even then, if the old black saint's lack of those commonplace accomplishments accounted, in any way, for his marvelous knowledge of the unseen world.

And father--father--was the greatest, the wisest, and the best man that ever lived. The boy wondered, sometimes, why the Bible did not tell about his father. Surely, in all the world, there was no other man so good as he. And, as for wisdom! There was nothing--nothing-- that father did not know! Always, when other men came to see them, there was talk of such strange things as "government" and "party" and "campaigns" and "senators" and "congressmen"--things that the boy did not in the least know about--but he knew that his father knew, which was quite enough, indeed, for a boy of his age to know.

The boy, in his Yesterdays, wondered greatly when he heard his father sometimes wish that he could be a boy again. To him, in the ignorance of his childhood, such a wish was very strange. Not until the boy had himself become a man and had learned to rightly value Ignorance did he understand his father's wish and in his heart repeat it.

But there was one in those Yesterdays, upon whose knowledge the boy looked in admiring awe, who taught him that which he could never outgrow. Very different from the wisdom of the hired man was the wisdom of this one. Very different was his knowledge from the knowledge of the old negro. Nor was his learning like, in any way, to the learning that made the boy's father so good and so wise among men.

But this leader did not often come openly to the boy's home. Always, when his mother saw the boy in the company of this one, she called him into the house, and often she explained to him that the one whom he so admired was a bad boy and that she did not wish her little son to play with him. So this intellectual leader of the Yesterdays was forced to come, stealthily, through the orchard, dodging from tree to tree, until, from behind the woodshed, he could, with a low whistle, attract the attention of his admiring disciple and beckon him to his side. Then the two would slip away over the brow of the hill or down behind the barn where, safe from mother's watchful eye, the boy could enjoy the companionship of this one whom Knowledge had so distinguished.

And often the older boy laughed at the Ignorance of his younger companion--laughed and sneered at him in the pride of superior learning--while the little boy felt ashamed and, filled with admiration for his forbidden friend, wondered if he would ever grow to be as wise. Scarcely could he hope, for instance, to be able, ever, to smoke and chew and swear in so masterful a way. And the little learner's face would beam with timid adoration and envy as he listened to the tales of wicked adventures so boastfully related by his teacher. Would he, could he, ever be so bold, so wise in knowledge of the world?

Poor little boy in the Yesterdays who knew nothing of the value of Ignorance! Poor boys in the grown up world--admiring and envying those who know more of evil than themselves!

So, always, secretly, the boy, as the years passed, gained the knowledge that makes men wish that they could be boys again. So, always, do men learn the value of Ignorance too late.

And then, as the man lived again in his Yesterdays, and, realizing in his manhood the value of Ignorance, wished that he could be a boy again, the little girl came to take her place in his intellectual life even as she took her place in all the life of his boyhood. Again he saw her wondering eyes as she stood with him in the stable door to watch the hired man among the horses. Again he felt her timid hand in his as he led her to a place where, safe from horns and heels, they could observe, together, the fascinating operation of milking. Together they listened to the words of strange wisdom and marveled at the knowledge of the barnyard scientist.

All that the boy learned from the old negro, of the fearsome creatures that inhabit the unseen world, he, in turn, gave to the little girl. And sometimes she even went with him on a pilgrimage to the cabin over the hill; there to gaze, half frightened, at the black-faced seer who had such store of awful wisdom.

The boy's pride in his father's superior goodness and wisdom she shared fully--because he was the father of the boy.

All the sweet lore of childhood was theirs in common. All the wise Ignorance of his Yesterdays she shared.

Only in the boy's forbidden friendship with that one who had such knowledge of evil the little girl did not share. This knowledge--the knowledge that was to go with him, even in his manhood years, and which, at last, would teach him the real value of Ignorance--the boy gained alone. Sadly, the man remembered how, sometimes, when the boy had stolen away to drink at that first muddy fountain of evil, he would hear her calling and would be held from answering by the jeers of his wicked teacher. But never when he was playing with the little girl did the boy answer the signal whistle of that one whose knowledge he envied but of whose friendship he was ashamed.

In his Yesterdays, the ignorance of his little girl mate was an anchor that held the boy from drifting too far in the current of evil. In his Yesterdays, the goodness and wisdom of his father was not a will-o'-the-wisp but, to the boy, a steady guiding light. What mattered, then, if the knowledge of the old negro *was* but a foolish mirage? What mattered if the hired man did *not know about fairies or if he did* know so many things that were not so? So it was that the man came to know the value of Ignorance. So it was that the man did not fall into the pit of saying: "There is only Ignorance."

And so it was, as he returned again from his Yesterdays, that day when even the reeking atmosphere of the city could not hide, altogether, the sweetness of the spring, that the memory of the little girl was with him even as the perfume of the season was in the air.

* * * * *

It was the time of the first flowers.

The woman had been out, somewhere, on a business errand and was returning to the place where she worked. A crowd had gathered, blocking the sidewalk, and she was forced to stop. Quickly, as if by magic, the people came running from all directions. The woman was annoyed. Her destination was only a few doors away and she had much work, still, to do before the remaining hours of the afternoon should be gone. She could not cross the street without going back for the traffic was very heavy. She faced about as if to retrace her steps, then, paused and turned again. The street would be open in a moment. It would be better to wait. Above the heads of the people she could see, already, the helmets of the police clearing the sidewalk. Pushing into the jam, she worked slowly forward.

Clang, clang, clang, with a rattle and clatter and crash, a patrol wagon swung up to the curb--so close that a spatter of mud from the gutter fell on the woman's skirt. The wagon wheeled and backed. The police formed a quick lane across the sidewalk. The crowd surged forward and carried the woman close against the blue coated barrier. Down the lane held by the officers of the law, so close to the woman that she could have touched them, came two poor creatures who were not ignorant of what is commonly called the world. They had seen life--so the world would have said. They were wise. They had knowledge of many things of which the woman, who shrank back from them in horror, knew nothing. Their haggard, painted, faces, their disheveled hair, their tawdry clothing, false jewels, and drunken blasphemies, drew a laugh from the crowd.

Upon the soul of the woman the laughter of the crowd fell like a demon laugh from the depths of hell. Almost she shrieked aloud her protest. Because she knew herself to be a woman, she almost shrieked aloud.

It was over in an instant. The patrol wagon rumbled away with its burden of woe. The crowd melted as magically as it had gathered. At the entrance of the building where she worked, the woman turned to look back, as though fascinated by the horror of that which she had seen. But, upon the surface of that sea of life, there was not the faintest ripple to mark the spot of the tragedy.

And the crowd had laughed.

The woman knew the character of that place so near the building in which she worked. Several times, each day, she passed the swinging doors of the saloon below and, always, she saw men going in and out. Many times she had caught glimpses of the faces of those who occupied the rooms above as they watched at the windows. When first she went to work she had known little of such things, but she was learning. Not because she wished to learn but because she could not help it. But the knowledge of such things had come to her so gradually that she had grown accustomed to knowing even as she came to know. She had become familiar with the fact without being forced to feel.

Perhaps, if the incident had occurred a few years later, when the woman's knowledge was more complete, she, herself, might have been able to laugh with the crowd. This knowledge that enables one so to laugh is, seemingly, much prized these days among those who have not the wisdom to value Ignorance.

The afternoon passed, as such afternoons must, and the woman did her work. What mattered the work that was being wrought in the soul of her womanhood--the work committed to her hands--the work that refused to recognize her womanhood--*that* work was done--and that is all that seems to matter. And, when her day's work was done, the woman boarded a car for her home.

It was an hour when many hundreds of toilers were going from their labor. So many hundreds there were that the cars could scarcely hold them and there were seats for only a few. Among those hundreds there were many who were proud of their knowledge of life. There were not many who knew the value of Ignorance. The woman who knew that she was a woman was crowded in a car where there was scarcely room for her to stand. She felt the rude touch of strangers--felt the bodies of strange men forced against her body--felt their limbs crushed against her limbs--felt their breath in her face--felt and trembled in frightened shame. In that car, crowded close against the woman, there were men whose knowledge of life was very great. By going to the lowest depths of the city's shame, where the foulest dregs of humanity settle, they had acquired that knowledge.

At first the woman had dreaded those evening trips from work in the crowded cars. But it was an everyday experience and she was becoming accustomed to it. She was learning not to mind. That is the horror of it--she was learning not to mind.

But this night it was different. The heart of her womanhood shrank within her trembling and afraid--cried out within her in protest at the outrage. In the fetid atmosphere of the crowded car; in the rough touch of the crushing bodies of sweating humanity; in the coarse, low, jest; she felt again the demon that she had heard in the laughter of the crowd. She saw again the horror of that which had leered at her from out the disfigured, drunken, faces of the poor creatures taken by the police.

Must she--must she learn to laugh that laugh with the crowd? Must she gain knowledge of the unclean, the vicious, the degrading things of life by actual contact? Was it not enough for her to know that those things were in the world as she knew that there was fever in the marsh lands; or must she go in person into the muck and mire of the swamps?

So it was that this woman, who knew herself to be a woman, did not crave Knowledge, but Ignorance. She prayed to be kept from knowing too much. And it was well for her so to pray. It was the highest wisdom. Because she knew her womanhood, she was afraid. She feared for her dream life that was to be beyond the old, old, door. She feared for that one who, perhaps, would come to cross with her the threshold for it was given this woman to know that only with one in whose purity of life she believed could she ever enter into the life of her dreams. The Master of Life, in His infinite wisdom, made the heart of womanhood divinely selfish. This woman knew that her dreams could never be for her save through her belief in the one who should ask her to go with him through that old, old, door. And the things that the woman found herself learning made it hard for her to believe in any man. The knowledge that was forced upon her was breeding doubt and distrust and denial of good. The realization of her womanhood's beautiful dream was possible only through wise Ignorance. She must fight to keep from learning too much.

And in the woman's fight there was this to help her: in the crowd that had laughed, her startled eyes had seen one or two who did not laugh--one or two there were whose faces were filled with pity and with shame. Always, in the crowded cars, there was some one who tried quietly to shield her from the press--some one who seemed to understand. It was this that helped. These men who knew the value of Ignorance kept the spark of her faith in men alive. The faith, without which her dreams would be idle dreams, impossible of fulfillment, was kept for her by those men who knew the value of Ignorance.

The woman went to her work the next morning with a heart that was heavy with dread and nerves that were quivering with fear. The brightness, the beauty, and the joy, of her womanhood, she felt to be going from her as the sunshine goes under threatening clouds. The blackness, the ugliness, and the sorrow, of life, she felt coming over her as fog rolls in from the sea. The faith, trust, and hope, that is the soul of womanhood was threatened by doubt, distrust, and despair. The gentleness, sensitiveness, and delicacy, that is the heart of womanhood was beset by coarseness, vulgarity, and rudeness. Could she harden her woman heart, steel her woman nerves, and make coarse her woman soul to withstand the things that she was forced to meet and know? And if she could--what then--would she gain or lose thereby? For the life of which she had dreamed, would she gain or lose?

It was nearly noon when a voice at her side said: "You are ill!"

It was a voice of authority but it was not at all unkind.

Turning, she looked up into his face and stammered a feeble denial. No, she was not ill.

But the kind eyes looked down at her so searchingly, so gravely, that her own eyes filled with tears.

"Come, come," said the voice, "this won't do at all. You must not lose your grip, you know. It will be all right to-morrow. Take the afternoon off and get out into the fresh air."

And something in his voice--something in his grave, steady, eyes--told her--made her feel that he understood. It helped her to know that this man of large affairs, of power and authority, understood.

So, for that afternoon, she went to a park in a distant part of the city to escape, for a few hours, the things that were crowding her too closely. Near the entrance of the park, she met a gray haired policeman who, looking at her keenly, smiled kindly and touched his hat; then, before she had passed from sight, he turned to follow leisurely the path that she had taken. Finding a quiet nook on the bank of a little stream that was permitted to run undisturbed by the wise makers of the park, the woman seated herself, while the policeman, unobserved by her, paused not far away to watch a group of children at play.

Perhaps it was the blue sky, unstained by the city smoke: perhaps it was the sunbeams that filtered through the leafy net-work of the trees to fall in golden flakes and patches on the soft green: perhaps it was the song that the little brook was singing as it went its merry way: perhaps it was the twittering, chirping, presence of the feathery folk who hopped and flitted so cheerily in and out among the shrubs and flowers--whatever it was that brought it about, the life that crowded her so closely drifted far, far, away. The city with its noisy clamor, with its mad rush and unceasing turmoil, was gone. The world of danger, and doubt, and fear, was forgotten. The woman lived again the days that were gone. The sky so blue above her head was the sky that arched her days of long ago. The sunshine that filtered through the trees was the same golden wealth that enriched the days of her childhood. The twittering, chirping, feathery, folk were telling the same old stories. The little brook that went so merrily on its way was singing a song of the Yesterdays.

They were free days--those Yesterdays--free as the days of the feathery folk who lived among the shrubs and flowers. There was none of the knowledge that, with distrust and doubt and despair, shuts in the soul. They were bright days--those Yesterdays--as bright as the sunlight that out of a clear sky comes to glorify the world. There was none of that dark and dreadful knowledge that shrouds the soul in gloom. And they were glad days--those Yesterdays--glad with the gladness of the singing brook. There was none of that knowledge that stains and saddens the heart.

The woman, sitting there so still by the little brook, did not notice a well dressed man who was strolling slowly through the park. A little way down the walk, the man turned, and again went slowly past the place where the woman sat. Once more he turned and this time seated himself where he could watch her. The man's face was not a good face. For a little while he watched the woman, then rising, was starting leisurely toward her when the gray haired policeman came suddenly into view around a turn in the path. The officer did not hesitate; nor was he smiling, now, as he stepped in front of the man. A few crisp words he spoke, in a low tone, and pointed with his stick. There was no reply. The fellow turned and slunk away while the guardian of the law, with angry eyes, watched him out of sight, then turned to look toward the woman. She had not noticed. The officer smiled and quietly strolled on down the path.

The woman had noticed neither the man nor her protector because she was far, far, away in her Yesterdays. She did not heed the incident because she was a little girl again, playing beside the brook that came across the road and made its winding way through the field just below the house. It was only a little brook, but beautifully clear and fresh, for it had come only a short distance from its birth place in a glen under the hill that she could see from her window. In some places, the long meadow grass, growing close down to the edge, almost touched above, making a cool, green, cradle arch through which the pure waters flowed with soft whispers as though the baby stream were crooning to itself a lullaby. In other stretches, the green willows bent far over to dip their long, slim, fingers in the slow current that crept so lazily through the flickering light and shade that it seemed scarce to move at all. And other places there were, where the streamlet chuckled and laughed over tiny pebbly bars in the sunlight or gurgled past where flags and rushes grew.

Again, with her dolls, the little girl played on the grassy bank; washing their tiny garments in the clear water and hanging them on the flags or willows to dry; resting often to listen to the fairy song the water sang; or to whisper to the brook the secrets of her childhood dreams. The drowsy air was full of the sweet, grassy, smell mingled with the odor of mint and the perfume of the willows and flags and warm moist earth. Gorgeous winged butterflies zigzagged here and there from flower to flower--now near for a little--then far away. Honeybees droned their hymns of industry the while they searched for sweet treasures. And now and then a tiny green frog would come out of a shadowy nook in the bank of the stream to see what the little girl was doing; or a bird would drop from out the blue sky for a drink or a bath in the pebbly shallows. And not far away--easily within call--mother sat on the shady porch, with her sewing, where she could watch over her little girl.

Dear, innocent, sheltered, protected, Yesterdays--when mother told her child all that was needful for her to know, and told her in a most tender, beautiful, way. Dear, blessed, Yesterdays--when love did not leave vice to teach the sacred truths of love--days that were days of blissful Ignorance--not vicious Ignorance but ignorance of the vicious. There was a wealth of Ignorance in those Yesterdays that is of more worth to womanhood, by far, than much knowledge of the world.

And often the boy would come, too, and, together, they would wade hand in hand in the clear flood, mingling their shouts and laughter with the music of their playmate brook, while the minnows darted to and fro about their bare legs; or, they would build brave dams and bridges and harbors with the bright stones; or, best of all, fashion and launch the ships of childhood.

Oh, childish ships of the Yesterdays! What precious cargoes they carried! What priceless treasures they bore to the far away port of dreams!

The little brook was a safe stream for the boy and the girl to play beside. Nor did they know, then, that their streamlet flowed on and on until it joined the river; and that the river, in its course, led it past great cities that poured into it the poisons and the filth of their sewers, fouling its bright waters, until it was unfit for children to play beside.

They did not know, *then*--but the woman knew, *now*.

And what--she thought as she came back from her Yesterdays--what of the boy who had played with her beside the brook? He, too, must have learned what happened to their brook. In learning, what had happened to him--she wondered--and wondering, she was afraid.

Because she was no longer ignorant, she was afraid for the mate of her Yesterdays. Not that she thought over to meet him again. She did not wish, now, to meet him for she was afraid. She would rather have him as he was in her Yesterdays.

Slowly the woman turned away from the quiet seat beside the brook. It was time for her to go.

Not far away, she passed the gray haired policeman, who again smiled and touched his hat.

Smiling in return she bade him: "Good afternoon."

"Good afternoon, Miss," he said, still smiling gravely. "Come again, Miss, when ye's want a breath of air that's pure and clean." May heaven bless, for the sweet sake of womanhood, all men who understand.

RELIGION

IT was springtime--blossoming time--mating time. The world was a riot of color and perfume and song.

Every twig that a few weeks before had been a bare, unsightly stick was now a miracle of dainty beauty. From the creek, below the little girl's house, the orchard hill appeared against the soft, blue, sky a wonderous, cumulus, cloud of fleecy whiteness flushed with a glow of delicate pink. The meadows and pastures were studded with stars of gold and pearl, of ruby and amethyst and silver. The fairy hands that had thrown over the wood a filmy veil of dainty color now dressed each tree and bush in robes of royal fabric woven from many tints of shimmering, shining, green.

Through the amber light above new turned furrows; amid the jewel glint of water in the sun; in the diamond sparkle of the morning; against the changing opal skies of evening; the bees and all their winged kin floated and darted, flashed and danced, and whirled, from flower to flower and field to field, from blossom to blossom and tree to tree, bearing their pollen messages of love and life while sweet voiced birds, in their brightest plumage, burdened the perfumed air with the passionate melody of their mating time.

All nature seemed bursting with eager desire to evidence a Creator's power. Every tint and color, every breath of perfume, every note of music, every darting flight or whirling dance, was a call to life--a challenge to love--an invitation to mate--a declaration of God. The world throbbed and exulted with the passion of the Giver of Life.

Life itself begat Religion.

Not the least of the Thirteen Truly Great Things of Life is Religion. Religion is an exaltation of Life or it is nothing. To exalt Life truly is to be most truly religious.

But the man, when he first awoke that morning, did not think of Religion. His first thought was a thought of lazy gratitude that he need not get up. It was Sunday. With a long sigh of sleepy content, he turned toward the wall to escape the too bright light that, from the open window, had awakened him and dozed again.

It was Sunday.

There are bitter cold, icy, snowy, Sundays in mid-winter when one hugs the cheerless radiator and, shivering in chilly discomfort, wishes that Sundays were months instead of days apart. There are stifling, sticky, sweltering. Sundays in midsummer when one prays, if he can pray at all, for the night to come. And there are blustering, rainy, sleety, dismal, Sundays in the fall when the dead hours go in funeral procession by and the world seems a gloomy tomb. But a Sunday in blossoming time! That is different! The very milk wagons, as they clattered, belated, down the street rattled a cheery note of fellowship and good will. The long drawn call of the paper boy had in it a hint of the joy of living. And the rumble of an occasional passing cab came like a deep undertone of peace.

The streets were nearly empty. The stores and offices, with closed doors, were deserted and still. A solitary policeman on the corner appeared to be meditating, indifferent to his surroundings. The few pedestrians to be seen moved leisurely and appeared as though in a mood for reflective thought and quiet interest in the welfare of their fellows. The hurrying, scrambling, jostling, rushing crowd; the clanging, crashing, roaring turmoil; the racking madness, the fierce confusion, the cruel selfishness of the week day world was as a dreadful dream in the night. In the hard fought battle of life, the world had called a truce, testifying thus to the place and power of Religion.

This is not to say that the world professes Religion; but it *is* to say that Religion possesses the world. In a thousand, thousand, forms, Religion possesses the world. In thoughts, in deeds, in words--in song and picture and story--in customs and laws and industries--in society, state, and school--in all of the Thirteen Truly Great Things of Life, Religion makes itself manifest and declares its power over men. If one proclaim himself without Religion then is its power made known in that one's peculiarity. If Religion did not possess the world, to scorn it would mark no one as different from his fellows, And this, too, is true: so imperial is the fact of Religion, that he who would deny it is forced to believe so firmly in his disbelief that he accepts the very thing he rejects, disguised in a dress of his own making, and thus bows down in worship before a God of his own creation.

To many, Sunday is a day of labor. To many others, it is a day of roistering and debauch. To some, it is a day of idleness and thoughtless pleasure. To some, it is a day of devotion and worship. But still, I say, that, whatever men, as individuals, may do with the day, the deserted streets, the silent stores, the closed banks, the empty offices, evidence that, to the world, this day is not as other days and give recognition--not to creeds and doctrines of warring sects indeed--but, to Religion.

Again the man awoke. Coming slowly out of his sleep and turning leisurely in his bed he looked through the open window at the day. And still he did not think of Religion.

Leisurely he arose and, after his bath, shaved himself with particular care. With particular care he dressed, not in the garb of every day, but in fresher, newer, raiment. Thus did he, even as the world, give unthinking testimony to the power and place of Religion.

Later, when the church bells sent their sweet voiced invitations ringing over the city, the man went to church. He did not go to church because he was a religious man nor because he was in a religious mood; he went because it was his habit to go occasionally. Even as most men sometimes go to church, so this man went. Nor did he, as a member of any religious organization, feel it his duty to go. He went as he had always gone--as thousands of others who, like himself, in habit of dress and manner were giving unconscious testimony to the power of Religion in the world, went, that day, to some place of public worship.

The streets of the city were now well filled with people. Yesterday, these same people, in the same streets, had rushed along with anxious, eager, strained, expressions upon their faces that told of nerves tense, minds intent, and bodies alert, in the battle they waged for daily bread, for gain, and for all the things that are held by men to be worth the struggle. To-morrow, these same people would again lose themselves in the fierce and strenuous effort of their lives. But to-day, they walked leisurely; they spoke calmly; they thought coolly; they had time to notice each other; to greet each other, to smile, to shake each others' hands. There were many children, too, who, dressed in their Sunday clothes, with clean faces and subdued manners, even as their parents, evidenced the power of Religion in the life of humankind. And, even as their parents, the children knew it not. They did not recognize the power of Religion in their lives.

The man did not think of the meaning of these things; though he felt it, perhaps, somewhat as he felt the warm life of the sun filled air: he sensed it, perhaps, as he sensed the beauty of the morning. He did not realize, then, how, in his Dreams, Religion had subtly manifested itself. He did not realize, that, in his Occupation, he was, every day, revealing the influence of Religion in his life. He had seen Religion but dimly when he had thought to follow the golden chain of Knowledge, link by link, to its hidden end. Dimly had he seen it when he was learning the value of Ignorance. And yet, in all of these things it had been even as it would be in all the things that were yet to come. No man can escape Religion. Man may escape particular forms of Religion, indeed, but Religion itself he cannot escape.

With many others the man entered a church. An usher gravely led him to a seat. I do not know what church it was to which the man went that morning nor does it, for my story, matter that I do not know. My story is not of churches nor of sects nor of creeds. This is my story: that the man came to realize in his life the power of Religion.

It may have been the beauty of the morning that did it; it may have been that the week just past was unusually hard and trying and that the day of rest, therefore, was more than usual, needed: or, perhaps, it was because the man had learned that he could never follow the golden chain of Knowledge to its hidden end and had come to know the value of Ignorance for Religion walks ever close to both Knowledge and Ignorance, hand in hand with each; whatever it was that brought it about, the man, that Sunday, came to realize the power of Religion in the world and in his own manhood life.

It was very quiet in the church but it was not a sad quietness. The people moved softly and, when they spoke at all, spoke in whispers but there was no feeling of death in the air; rather was there a feeling of life--a feeling of life, too, that was very unlike the feeling of life in a crowded place of business or amusement. The sweet, plaintively pleading, tones of the organ trembled in the air. The glorious sunshine came through the stained glass windows softened and subdued. Here and there heads were bowed. The people became very still. And, in the stillness, the man felt strongly the spirit of the day and place. The organ tones increased in volume. The choir filed in. The preacher entered. The congregation arose to sing an old triumphant hymn.

The man did not sing, but, as he listened to the music and followed the words of the hymn, he smiled. The people were singing about unknowable things--of streets of gold and gates of pearl--of crowns and harps and the throne of God.

All his life, the man had known that hymn but he had never before thought of it just as he thought of it that morning. He looked about at the people who were singing. Who were they? Uneducated, irresponsible, fanatical dreamers of no place or importance in the week day world? No indeed! They were educated, responsible, practical, hard headed, clear brained, people of power and influence--and--the man smiled again--they were singing about unknowable things. For the first time in his life, the man wondered at the strangeness of it all.

When the minister prayed, the man listened as he had never listened to a prayer before. He felt baffled and bewildered as though he had wandered into a strange land, among strange people, of whose customs he was ignorant, and whose language he could neither speak nor understand. Who was this man who seemed on such familiar terms with the Infinite? Upon what did he base his assurance that the wealth of blessings he asked for himself and his people would be granted or even heard? Had he more than finite mind that he could know the Infinite?

The sermon that followed was largely a sermon about unknowable things. It was full of beautiful, helpful, thoughts about things that it was impossible for anyone to really know anything about. Very familiar were the things that the minister said that morning. Since his childhood, the man had heard them over and over many times; but he had never before thought of them in just that way.

The sermon was finished and the beautifully mysterious and impressive words of the benediction were spoken as the people stood with bowed heads, hushed and still. Again the deep tones of the organ trembled in the air as the crowd poured forth from the building into the street.

The man was thoughtful and troubled. He felt as one, who, meeting an old friend after many years, finds him changed beyond recognition. He was as one visiting, after years of absence, his old home to find the familiar landmarks all gone with the years. He was sadly conscious that something had gone out of his life--that something exceedingly precious had been taken away from him and that it could never be replaced.

Seriously, sadly, the man asked himself: must his belief in Religion go as his faith in fairies had gone? Was Religion, after all, but a beautiful game played by the grown up world, even as children play? And if, indeed, his faith must go because songs and prayers and sermons have to do so largely with unknowable things, what of the spirit of the world expressed in the day that is so set apart from all other days? Sunday is a fact knowable enough. And the atmosphere of the church is another fact as knowable as the atmosphere of a race track, a foundry, or a political convention. And the fruits of Religion in the lives of men--these are as clearly knowable as the fruits of drunkenness, or gambling, or licentiousness. The man was as sure of the fruits of Religion as he was sure that the sun was shining--that the day, so warm and bright, was unlike the cold, hard, stormy, days of winter. And still--and still--the songs and prayers and sermons about unknowable things--must his belief in Religion go as his faith in fairies had gone?

Unknowable things? Yes--as unknowable as that mysterious something that colors the trees and plants and flowers with tints of infinite shadings--as unknowable as that which puts the flavor in the peach, the strength in the corn, the perfume in the rose--as unknowable as the awful force that reveals itself in the lightning flash or speaks in the rolling thunder--as unknowable as the mysterious hand that holds the compass needle to the north and swings the star worlds far beyond the farthest reach of the boasting eye of Science. Unknowable? Yes--as unknowable as that which lies safe hidden behind the most commonplace facts of life--as unknowable indeed, as Life itself.

"Nature," said the man, in answer to himself, and smiled at the foolishness of his own answer. Is nature then so knowable? Are all her laws revealed; all her secrets known; all her ways understood; all her mysteries made clear? Do the wise men, after all, know more of nature than they do of God? Do they know more of earth than of heaven? Do they know more of a man's mind than they do of his soul? And yet--and yet--does one refuse to live because he cannot understand the mystery of life? Does one deny the earth because the secrets of Mature are unknowable? Does one refuse to think because thoughts are not material things--because no one has ever seen a thought to say from whence it came or whither it went?

Disbelief demands a knowledge as exact as that demanded by belief. To deny the unknowable is as impossible as to affirm it. If it be true that man knows too much to believe in miracles these days, it is just as true that he does not know enough to disbelieve in them. And, after all, there is no reason why anyone should believe in miracles; neither is there any reason why one should disbelieve in them.

Every altar is an altar to an unknown God. But man does not refuse to believe in bread because he cannot understand the mystery of the wheat field. One believes in a garden, not because he knows how, from the same soil, water, and air, Nature produces strawberries, potatoes, sweet corn, tomatoes, or lettuce, but because fresh vegetables are good. The hungry man neither believes nor disbelieves but sits down to the table and, if he be a right minded man, gives thanks to the God of gardens who, in ways so unknowable, gives such knowable gifts to man.

Nor was the man, at this time, able to distinguish clearly between Religion and the things that men have piled about and hung upon Religion. Therefore was he troubled about his waning belief and worried because of his growing doubt. He did not wish to doubt; he wished to believe.

In all these many years, through intellectual pride or selfish ambition, because of an earnest but mistaken purpose to make clear, or in a pious zeal to emphasize, men have been piling things about and hanging things upon Religion; and, always, they have insisted that this vast accumulation of things *is* Religion.

These things that men have hung upon Religion are no more a part of Religion than the ivy that grows upon the stone wall of a fortress is a part of the nation's defensive strength. These things that men have piled about Religion belong to it no more than a pile of trash dumped at the foot of a cliff belongs to the everlasting hills. But these traditions and customs of men, with their ever multiplying confusions of doctrines and creeds and sects, beautiful as they are, hide Religion even as the ivy hides the wall. Even as the accumulated trash of the ages piled at the foot of the cliff is of interest to the archaeologist and the seeker after curious junk, so these things that men have piled about Religion are of interest. But the observer, in admiration of the ivy, is in danger of ignoring the stern reality of the fortress. The curious digger in the pile of trash, if his interest be great, heeds not the grandeur of the cliff that towers above his head.

That afternoon the man went for a long walk. He wished to think out, if he could, the things that troubled him.

Without plan on his part, his walk led toward a quarter of the city where he had never been before and where he came at last to an old cemetery. The ancient iron gates, between their vine clad columns of stone, were invitingly open and within the enclosure were great trees that locked their green arms above the silent, grass grown, graves as though in sheltering kindness for the dead. Tempted by the beauty of the place the man entered, and, in the deep shade of the old trees, screened from the road by their mossy trunks, found a seat. Here and there, among the old graves under the trees, a few people moved slowly; pausing often to decipher the inscriptions upon the leaning and fallen tombstones. So old was that ancient burying place that there was left among the living no one to keep the flowers upon the graves and visitors came only from idle curiosity.

And it was so, that, as the man sat there under the quiet old trees, the graves with their leaning and fallen tombstones, or, perhaps, the day itself, led his mind back to those companion graves that marked the passing of his boyhood--back to father and mother and to their religion--back to the religion of his Yesterdays. And the week of toil and strife, of struggle and of storm, slipped far, far, away. The disturbing questions, the doubt and the uncertainty of the morning, raised as the fogs lift to leave the landscape clear.

It was such a little way from the boy's home to the church that, when the weather was fine, they always walked. And surely no day could have been finer than that Sunday to which the man went back. As the boy, all washed and combed and dressed in his Sunday best, sat on the big gate post waiting for his father and mother, it seemed to him that every living thing about the place knew what day it was. In the pasture across the road, the horses, leisurely cropping the new grass, paused often to lift their heads and look about with an air of kindly interest in things to which they would have given no heed at all had they been in week day harness. And one old gray, finding an inviting spot, lay down to roll--got up--and, because it felt so good, lay down again upon his other side; and then, as if regretting that he had no more sides to rub, stretched himself out with such a huge sigh of content that the boy on the gate post laughed; whereat the horse raised his head and looked at him as though to say: "Little boy, don't you know that it is Sunday?" Under the big elm, in the corner of the pasture, the cows stood, with half closed eyes, chewing their cuds with an air of pious meditation. The hens strolled sedately about singing solemnly: ca-w-w, ca-w-w, ca-w-w, and the old red rooster, standing on tiptoe, flapped his wings as if to crow then checked himself suddenly and looked around as if to say: "Bless me, I nearly forgot what day it is!" Then the clear, mellow, tones of the church bell floated across the little valley and the boy's parents came out of the house. The dog, stretched at full length on the porch, lifted his head but did not offer to follow. He, too, seemed to know, thought the boy as he climbed down from the post to walk soberly away with his parents.

Before they reached the lower end of the garden, the little girl with her mother and uncle came out of their house and, at the gate, waited for them while the little girl waved her hand in greeting. Then the two men and the two women walked on ahead and, as the boy and girl followed, the boy, looking shyly at his companion, saw the sunlight on her soft, brown, hair that was so prettily arranged with a blue ribbon--saw the merry eyes under the broad brim of her best hat--saw the flushed, softly rounded, cheek with the dimple, the curve of the red lips, and the dainty chin--saw her dress so clean and white and starched--saw and wondered if the angels in heaven could be more beautiful than this little girl.

So they went, that Sunday, down the hill, across the creek, and up the gentle slope beyond, until they came to the cross roads where the white church stood under the old elm and maple trees. Already there were many teams standing under the sheds or tied to the hitch racks along the side of the road. And by the roads that led away in four directions, through the fields and meadows and pastures of the farms, other country folk were coming from their homes and their labors to worship the God of seedtime and harvest.

There were no ushers in that church of the Yesterdays for there would be no strangers save those who would come with their friends; but the preacher himself was at the door to greet his people or was moving here and there among them, asking with care for the absent ones. Neither was there a great organ to fill the air with its trembling tones; but, at the humble instrument that served as well, the mother of the little girl presided, while the boy's father led the country choir. And the sunlight of that Sunday streamed through the open windows, softened only by the delicate traceries of gently waving branches and softly rustling leaves.

And in the songs and prayers and sermons of that worship in the Yesterdays, the boy heard the same unknowable things that the man had heard that morning in the city church. Among those people, the boy felt stirring the same spirit that had moved the man. The old preacher was long ago resting in the cemetery on the hill, with the boy's parents, the mother of the little girl, and many, many, others of his flock. A new and more modern minister would be giving, now, to the children of that old congregation, the newest and most modern things that theologians do not know about Religion. But the same old spirit would be there still; doing the same work for the glory of the race. And the boy in the Yesterdays, as he listened to the songs and prayers and sermons, had wondered in his heart about the things he heard--even as the man, he had asked himself many unanswerable questions... But there had been no doubt in the questions of the boy. There had been no disbelief in his wonder. Because the girl's mother played the organ--because the boy's father sang in the choir--because his mother and the little girl were there beside him--the boy believed that which he could not understand.

"By their fruits"--it is a text as good for grown up children as for boys and girls.

What the preachers say about Religion matters little after all. It is the fathers and mothers and the little girls who keep the faith of the world alive. The *words* of those sermons and prayers and songs in his Yesterdays would go with the boy no farther than the church door; but that which was in the hearts of those who sang and preached and prayed--that which song and sermon and prayer attempted but could not express--*that* would go with the boy through all the years of his life. From *that* the man could never get wholly away. It became as much a part of him as his love for his parents was a part.

When church and Sunday school were over the boy went home to the miracle of the Sunday dinner. And, even as the unknowable things upon the Sunday dinner table contributed to his manhood's physical strength and health, so the things expressed by the day that is set apart from all other days contributed to that strength of manhood that is more vital than the strength of bone and muscle and nerve and sinew. In the book wherein it is written: "Man shall not live by bread alone," it is written, also: "Except ye become as little children."

Slowly the man arose. Slowly and regretfully he turned to leave his place under the great trees that, in the solemn, quiet, twilight of the old cemetery, locked their arms protectingly above the dead.

"Except ye become as little children."

Must men in Religion be always trying to grow up? Are the wisest and the greatest among scholars nearer the secrets of the unknowable power, that, through Religion, possesses the world, than the unthinking children are? As the man in the late afternoon went out through the ancient iron gates, between the vine covered columns of stone, he knew that his belief in Religion would not go as his faith in fairies had gone. Because of those companion graves and all that they meant to him--because of the little girl in his Yesterdays--his faith in Religion would not go.

* * * * *

The woman, alone in her room, sat at the open window looking out over the city. The long, spring, Sunday was drawing to its close. Above the roofs of the houses across the street, above the towering stories of the buildings in the down town districts, above factory chimneys, church steeples, temple dome, and cathedral spire, she saw the evening sky light with the glory of the passing day. Over a triumphant arch in the west, through which the sun had gone, a mighty cloud curtain of purple was draped, fold on fold, all laced and looped with silver and edged with scarlet flame. Above the curtain, far flung across the wide sky, banners of rose and crimson and gold flashed and gleamed; while, marching in serried ranks, following the pathway of the sun, went innumerable thousands of cloud soldiers in their uniforms of light. Slowly the procession passed--the gleaming banners vanished--the marching armies disappeared--the curtain in the west was drawn close. The woman at the window watched until the last of the light was gone and, in the still sky above, the stars hung motionless. Like a benediction, the sweet mystery of twilight had come upon the land. Like a softly breathed blessing from heaven, the night had come.

Because of the experience through which she had passed in the week just gone, that day, dedicated to Religion, had held for the woman a new meaning.

Looking into the darkness that hid the city from her eyes she shuddered. There were so many there to whom the night came not as a blessing, but as a curse. Out there, in the soft darkness into which the woman looked, dreadful crimes were being committed, horrid deeds were being planned. Out there, in the quiet night, wretched poverty, gaunt pain, and loathsome disease were pulling down their victims. Out there, in the blackness, hideous licentiousness, beastly passion, debasing pleasure were stalking their prey. Out there, murderers of souls were lying in wait; robbers of hearts were creeping stealthily; slayers of purity were watching; killers of innocence were lurking. To the woman at the window, that night, the twinkling lights of the city were as beacon fires on the outskirts of hell.

And to-morrow--to-morrow--she must go down into that hell. All that was there in the darkness, she must see, she must know, she must feel. All those things of evil would be watching her, crowding her, touching her, hungering for her; placing pitfalls in her way; longing for her to slip; waiting for her to fall; testing her, trying her, always ready with a damnable readiness; always hoping with a hellish hope. Into that she must go--even into that--this woman, who knew herself to be a woman, must go.

And what--what--of her dreams? Could she, she asked herself that night, could she go into that life, day after day, and still have a heart left for dreaming? Against the unclean strength that threatened her, where would she find the strength to keep her womanhood pure and strong for the holy mission of womanhood?

Clear and sweet from out the darkness of the night came the sound of a bell. Then another, and another, and another, until, from every quarter of the city, their music came, as though in answer to her question. Some, near at hand, rang loud, triumphant, peals as though rejoicing over victories already won; others, farther away, in softer tones, seemed to promise strength for present need; while still others, in more distant places, sounding soft and far away, seemed to gently warn, to beckon, to call, to plead. Lifting her tear filled eyes from the lights of the streets the woman looked at the stars, and, so looking, saw, lifting into the sky, the church spires of the city.

In a little, the music of the bells ceased. But the woman, at the window, sat still with her face upturned to the stars.

Gone, now, were the city lights that to her had seemed as beacon fires on the outskirts of hell. Gone, now, the horrors of that life to which night comes not as a benediction. Gone, now, her fears for her dreams. The woman lived again a Sunday evening in her Yesterdays.

It may have been the flaming glory of the sky; it may have been the music of the bells; it may have been the stars--whatever it was--the woman went again into the long ago. Once again she went back into her Yesterdays--to a Sunday evening in her Yesterdays.

The little girl was on the front porch of her home with mother. The sun was going down behind the great trees in the old churchyard at the cross roads while, across the valley, the voice of the bell was calling the people to evening worship. And, with the ringing of the bell, the boy and his mother came to sit with them while the men were gone to church.

Then, while the mothers, seated in their easy chairs, talked in low tones, the boy and the girl, side by side, on the steps of the porch, watched the light go out of the sky and tried to count the stars as they came. As the twilight deepened, the elms in the pasture across the road, the maples along the drive, and the willows down by the creek, became shadowy and indistinct. From the orchard, an owl sent forth his quavering call and was answered by his mate from the roof of the barn. Down in the shadow of the little valley, a whip-poor-will cried plaintively, and, now and then, a bat came darting out of the dusk on swift and silent wings. And there, in the darkness across the valley, shone the single light of the church. The children gave up trying to count the stars and grew very still, as, together, they watched the lights of the church. Then one of the mothers laughed, a low happy laugh, and the children began telling each other about God.

Many things the boy and the girl told each other about God. And who is there to say that the things they told were not just as true as many things that older children tell? Though, I suppose, as the boy and girl did not quarrel or become angry with each other that Sunday evening, their talk about God could scarcely be considered orthodox. Their service under the stars was not at all regular, I know. With childish awe and reverence--with hushed voices--they only told each other about God. They did not discuss theology--they were not church members--they were only children.

Then, by and by, the father and uncle came, and, with his parents, the boy went home, calling through the dark, as he went, many good nights--each call sounding fainter and farther away. And, when she could neither hear nor make him hear more, the little girl went with her mother into the house, where, when she was ready for bed, she knelt to pray that old familiar prayer of the Yesterdays--forgetting not in her prayer to ask God to bless and keep the boy.

Oh, childish prayers of the Yesterdays! Made in the strength of a childish faith, what power divine is in them to keep the race from death! Oh, childish understanding of God, deep grounded in that wisdom to which scholars can never attain! Does the Master of Life still set little children among His disciples in vain?

The woman no longer feared that which lay in the darkness of the city. She knew, now, that she would have strength to keep the treasures of her womanhood safe for him should he come to lead her into the life of her dreams. She knew, now, what it was that would help her--that would enable her to keep that which Life had committed to her.

As she turned from the window, strength and peace were in her heart. As she knelt beside her bed to pray, her prayer was that prayer of her Yesterdays. The prayer of a child it was--the prayer of a woman who knows that she is a woman it was also.

TRADITION

IT was summer time--growing time.
The children of the little brown birds that had nested in the hedge near the cherry tree, that year, were flying now, quite easily, away from their little brown mother's counsel and advice. Even to the top of the orchard hill, they went in search of brave adventure, rejoicing recklessly in their freedom. But, for the parent birds, the ties of the home in the hedge were still strong. And, every day, they examined with experienced eyes the cherries, that, on the near by tree, were fast nearing ripening time.

With every gesture expressing more clearly than any spoken word his state of mind, the man jerked down the top of his desk, slammed the door, jabbed the elevator bell, and strode grimly out of the building.

The man's anger was not one of those flash like bursts of wrath, that, passing as quickly as they come, leave the sky as clear as though no storm had crossed it. Nor was it the slow kindling, determined, anger, that, directed against a definite object, burns with steady purpose. It was rather that sullen, hopeless, helpless rage, that, finding nothing to vent itself upon, endures even while recognizing that its endurance is in vain. It was the anger of a captive, wild thing against the steel bars of its cage, which, after months of effort, it has found too strong. It was the anger of an explorer against the impassable crags and cliffs of a mountain range that bars his path. It was the anger of a blind man against the darkness that will not lift.

The man's work demanded freedom and the man was not free. In his dreams, at the beginning of his manhood, he had thought himself free to work out his dreams. He had said to himself: "Alone, in my own strength, I will work. Depending upon no man, I will be independent. Limited only by myself, I will be free." He said this because he did not, then, know the strength of the bars. He had not, at that time, seen the mountain range. He had not faced the darkness that would not lift. Difficulties, hardships, obstacles, dangers, he had expected to face, and, in his strength, to overcome. But the greatest difficulty, the severest hardship, the most trying obstacle, the gravest danger, he had not foreseen.

Little by little, as the days and months had passed and the man had made progress in his work, this thing had made itself felt. Little by little, this thing had forced itself upon him until, at last, he was made to realize the fact that he was not independent of but dependent upon all men. He found that he was limited not alone by himself but by others. He understood, now, that he was not free to work out his dreams. He saw, now, that the thing most difficult to overcome--the thing that forbade his progress and refused him freedom--was Tradition. On every side he met this: "It has never been done; it, therefore, can never be done. The fathers of our fathers believed this, therefore we must believe it. This has always been, therefore this must always be. Others do this, think this, believe this, therefore you must so do and think and believe." The man found, that, beyond a point which others could see, others denied him the right to go. The established customs and habits of others fixed the limit of the progress he could make with the approval of the world.

At first he had laughed--secure in his own strength, he had laughed contemptuously. But that was because he did not then realize the power of this thing. Later he did not laugh. He became angry with a sullen, hopeless, helpless, rage that accomplished nothing--that could accomplish nothing--but only weakened the man himself. As one shut in a cell exhausts himself beating against the walls, so he wearied himself.

Not until he was in the full swing of his work had this thing come upon him in force. At the beginning of his manhood life, when, in the strength of his first manhood dreams he had looked out upon the world as a conquering emperor upon the field of a coming battle, he had not seen this thing. When he was crying out to the world for something to do this thing had not made itself felt. Not until he had made noticeable progress--not until he was in the full swing of his work--did he find himself forced to reckon with what others had done or said or thought or believed.

And never had the man felt his own strength as he felt it now when face to face with this thing against which his strength seemed so helpless. If only he could have freedom! He asked nothing but that. As in the beginning he had asked of the world only room and something to do, he asked now only for freedom to do. And the world granted him the freedom of the child who is permitted to play in the yard but must not go outside the fence. He was free to do his work--to play out his dreams--only so far as the established customs and fixed habits--Tradition--willed. "Beyond the fence that shuts in the familiar home ground," said the world, "you must not go. If you dare climb over the fence--if you dare go out of the yard," said the world, "I will punish you--I will ridicule you, condemn you, persecute you, ostracize you. I will brand you false, a self-seeker, a pretender, a charlatan, a trickster, a rogue. I will cry you unsafe, dangerous, a menace to society and the race, an evil to all that is good, an unspeakable fool. Stay in the yard," said the world, "and you may do what you like."

Even in matters of personal habits and taste, the man found that he was not free. In his dress; in the things he ate and drank; in his pleasures; in the books he read, the plays he attended, the pictures he saw, the music he heard, he found that he was expected to obey the mandates of the world--he found that he was expected to conform to Tradition--to the established customs and habits of others. In religion, in politics, in society, in literature, in art--as in his work--the world said: "Don't go outside the yard."

I do not know what work it was that the man was trying to do. It does not matter what his work was. But this I know: in every work that man, since the beginning, has tried to do, man has been hindered as this man was hindered--man has been denied as this man was denied, freedom. Tradition has always blocked the wheels of progress. The world has moved ahead always in spite of the world. Just as the world has always crucified its saviors, so, always, it has hindered and held back its leaders.

And this, too, I know: after the savior is crucified, those who nail him to the cross accept his teaching. While the world hinders and holds back its leaders, it always follows them.

But the man did not think of this that day when he left the

scene of his labor in such anger. He thought only of that which he was trying to do. When he went back to his work, the next day, he was still angry and with his anger, now, came discontent, doubt, and fear, to cloud his vision, to clog his brain and weaken his heart.

A friend, at lunch, said: "You look fagged, knocked out, done up, old man. You've been pegging away too long and too steadily. Why don't you let up for awhile? Lay off for a week or two. Take a vacation."

Again and again, that hot, weary, afternoon, the words of the man's friend came back to him until, by evening, he was considering the suggestion seriously. "Why not?" he asked himself. He was accomplishing little or nothing in his present mood. Why not accept the friendly advice? Perhaps--when he came back--perhaps, he could again laugh at the world that denied him freedom.

So he came to considering places and plans. And, as he considered, there was before him, growing always clearer as he looked, the scenes of his boyhood--the old home of his childhood--the place of his Yesterdays. There were many places of interest and pleasure to which the man might go, but, among them all, there was no place so attractive as the place of his Yesterdays. There was nothing he so wished to do as this: to go back to the old home and there to be, for a little while, as nearly as a man could be, a boy again.

If the man had thought about it, he would have seen in this desire to spend his vacation at the old home something of the same force that so angered him by hindering his work. But the man did not think about it. He wrote a letter to see if he might spend two weeks with the people who were living in the house where he was born and, when the answer came assuring him a welcome, quickly made his arrangements to go.

With boyish eagerness, he was at the depot a full half hour before the time for his train. While he waited, he watched the crowd, feeling an interest in the people who came and went in the never ending profession that he had not felt since that day when he had first come to the city to work out his dreams among men. In the human tide that ebbed and flowed through this world gateway, he saw men of wealth and men of poverty--people of culture and position who had come or were going in Pullman or private cars and illiterate, stupid, animal looking, emigrants who were crowded, much like cattle, in the lowest class. There were business men of large affairs; countrymen with wondering faces; shallow, pleasure seekers; artists and scholars; idle fools; vicious sharks watching for victims; mothers with flocks of children clinging to their skirts; working girls and business women; chattering, laughing, schoolgirls; and wretched creatures of the outcast life--all these and many more.

And, as he watched, perhaps because he was on his vacation, perhaps because of something in his heart awakened by the fact that he was going to his boyhood home, the man felt, as he had never felt before, his kinship with them all. With wealth and poverty, with culture and illiteracy, with pleasure and crime, with sadness and joy, as evidenced in the lives of those who passed in the crowd, the man felt a sympathy and understanding that was strangely new. And, more than this, he saw that each was kin to the other. He saw that, in spite of the wide gulf that separated the individuals in the throng, there was a something that held them all together--there was a force that influenced all alike--there was a something common to all. In spite of the warring elements of society; in spite of the clashing forces of business; in spite of the conflicting claims of industry represented in the throng; the man recognized a brotherhood, a oneness, a kinship, that held all together. And he felt this with a strange feeling that he had always known that it was there but had never recognized it before.

The man did not realize that this was so because he was not thinking of the people in their relation to his work. He did not know, that, because his heart and mind were intent upon the things of his Yesterdays, he saw the world in this new light. He did not, then, understand that the force which hindered and hampered him in his work--that denied him the full freedom he demanded--was the same force that he now felt holding the people together. Even as they all, whether traveling in Pullman, private car, or emigrant train, passed over the same rails, so they all, in whatever class they traveled on the road of Life, were guided by the Traditions--the established customs--the fixed habits--that are common to their race or nation. And the strength of a people, as a people, is in this oneness--this force that makes them one--the Traditions and customs and habits of life that are common to all. It is the fences of the family dooryards that hold the children of men together and make the people of a race or nation one.

So it was that the man, knowing it not, left his work behind and went, for strength and rest, back to the scenes of his Yesterdays in obedience to the command of the very thing that, in his work, had stirred him to such rage. For what, after all, are Traditions and customs and habits but a going back into the Yesterdays.

As the train left the city farther and farther behind, the man's thoughts kept pace with the fast flying wheels that were bearing him back to the scenes of his childhood. From the present, he retraced his steps to that day when he had dreamed his first manhood dreams and to those hard days when he was asking of the world only something to do. As, step by step, he followed his way back, incidents, events, experiences, people, appeared, even as from the car window he caught glimpses of the whirling landscape, until at last he saw, across the fields and meadows familiar to his childhood, the buildings of the old home, the house where the little girl had lived, the old church, and the orchard hill where he had sat that day when the smoke of a distant train moving toward the city became to him a banner leading to the battle front. Then the long whistle announced the station. Eagerly the man collected his things and, before the train had come to a full stop, swung himself to the depot platform where he was met by his kindly host.

As they drove past the fields and pastures, so quiet after the noisy city, the man grew very still. Past the little white church among its old trees at the cross roads; down the hill and across the creek; and slowly up the other side of the valley they went: then past the house where the little girl had lived; and so turned in, at last, to the home of that boy in the Yesterdays. And surely it was no discredit to the man that, when they left him alone in his old room to prepare for the evening meal, he scarce could see for tears.

Scenes of childhood! Memories of the old home! Recollections of the dear ones that are gone! No more can man escape these things of the Yesterdays than he can avoid the things of to-day. No more can man deny the past than he can deny the present. Tradition is to men as a governor to an engine; without its controlling power the race would speed quickly to its own destruction. One of the Thirteen Truly Great Things of Life is Tradition.

For two happy, healthful, restful, strengthening, inspiring weeks, the man lived, so far as a man can live, in his Yesterdays. In the cool shade of the orchard that once was an enchanted wood; under the old apple tree ship beside the meadow sea; on the hill where, astride his rail fence war horse, the boy had directed the battle and led the desperate charge and where the man had dreamed the first of his manhood dreams; in the garden where the castaway had lived on his desert island; in the yard near mother's window where the boy had built the brave play house for the little girl next door; in the valley, below where the little girl lived, beside the brook that in its young life ran so pure and clear; at the old school house in the edge of the timber; in the ancient cemetery, beside the companion graves; through the woods and fields and pastures; beside the old mill pond with its covered bridge; the man lived again those days of the long ago.

But, in the places of his Yesterdays, the man found, already, many changes. The houses and buildings were a little more weather-beaten, with many of the boards in the porch floors and steps showing decay. The trees in the orchard were older and more gnarled with here and there gaps in their ranks. The fences showed many repairs. The little schoolhouse was almost shabby and, with the wood cleared away, looked naked and alone. The church, too, was in need of a fresh coat of white. And there were many new graves in the cemetery on the hill. As time had wrought changes in the man himself, even so had it altered the scenes of his boyhood. Always, in men and in things, time works changes.

But it is not the changes wrought by time that harms. These come as the ripening of the fruit upon the tree. It is the sudden, violent, transformations that men are ever seeking to make, both in things and in themselves, that menace the ripening life of the race. It is well, indeed, for the world to hold fast to its Traditions. It is well to cling wisely to the past.

Nor did the man live again in his Yesterdays alone. He could not. Always, she was there--his boyhood mate--the little girl who lived next door.

But the opening in the hedge that, at the lower end of the garden, separated the boy's home from the home of the little girl, was closed. Long and carefully the man searched; smiling, the while, at a foolish wish in his heart that time would leave that little gate of the Yesterdays always open. But the ever growing branches had woven a thick barrier across the green archway hiding it so securely that, to the man, no sign was left to mark where it had been.

With that foolish regret still in his heart, the man asked, quite casually, of the people who were living in the house if they knew aught about his playmate of the Yesterdays.

They could tell him very little; only that she lived in a city some distance from his present home. What she was doing; whether married or alone; they could not say.

And the man, as he stood, with bared head, under the cherry tree in the corner near the hedge, told himself that he was glad that the people could tell him nothing. In his busy, grown up, life there was no room for a woman. In his battle with the things that challenged his advance, he must be free to fight. It was better for him that the little girl lived only in his Yesterdays. The little girl who had helped him play out his boyhood dreams must not hinder him while he worked out the dreams of his manhood. That is what the man told himself as he stood, with bared head, under the cherry tree. With the memory of that play wedding and that kiss in his heart, he told himself *that*!

I wonder, sometimes, what would happen if men should chance to discover how foolish they really are.

No doubt, the man reflected--watching the pair of brown birds as they inspected the ripening cherries--no doubt she has long ago forgotten those childish vows. Perhaps, in the grown up world, she has even taken new and more binding vows. Would he ever, he wondered, meet one with whom he could make those vows again? Once he had met one with whom he thought he wished to make them but he knew, now, that he had been mistaken. And he knew, too, that it was well that he had found his mistake in time. Somehow, as he stood there again under the cherry tree, the making of such vows seemed to the man more holy, more sacred, than they had ever seemed before. Would he dare--He wondered. Was there, in all the world, a woman with whom he could--The man shrugged his shoulders and turned away. Yes, indeed, it was much better that she lived only in his Yesterdays. And still--still--in the man's heart there was regret that Time had closed that gateway of his Yesterdays.

And often, in the twilight of those evenings, after a day of wandering about the place, visiting old scenes, or talking with the long time friends of his people, the man would recall the traditions of his family; hearing again the tales his father would tell by the winter fireside or listening to the stories that his mother would relate on a Sunday or a stormy afternoon. Brave tales they were--brave tales and true stories of the man's forbears who had lived when the country was young and who had played no small part in the nation's building. And, as he recalled these traditions of his people, the man's heart thrilled with loyal pride while he determined strongly to keep the splendid record clean. As a sacred heritage, he would receive these traditions. As a holy duty he would be true to that which had been.

Reluctantly, but with renewed strength and courage, when the time came for his going, the man set his face away from his Yesterdays--set it again toward his work--toward the working out of his dreams. And, as he went, there was for the thing that checked his progress something more than anger--for the thing that forced him to go slowly there was patience.

Standing on the rear platform, as his train moved slowly away past an incoming train that had just pulled onto a siding, the man saw the neighbor who lived next door to his old home drive hurriedly up. The man in the carriage waved his hand and the man on the moving train, answering in like manner, wondered idly what had brought the neighbor there. Surely he had not come to bid one who was almost a stranger good-bye. And, strangely enough, as the man watched from the window for a last view of the scenes of his Yesterdays, there was in his heart, again, regret that the little opening in the hedge was closed.

* * * * *

The city was sweltering in a summer heat wave. The sun shone through a dingy pall of vile smoke with a sickly, yellow, glare. From the pavement and gutter, wet by the sprinkling wagons, in a vain effort to lay the dust, a sticky, stinking, steam lifted, filling the nostrils and laving the face with a combination of every filthy odor. The atmosphere fairly reeked with the smell of sweating animals, perspiring humanity, rotting garbage, and vile sewage. And, in the midst of the hot filth, the people moved with languid, feeble manner; their faces worn and pallid; their eyes dull and weary; their voices thin and fretful.

The woman's heart was faint with the weight of suffering that she was helpless to relieve. Her quivering nerves shrieked with the horror of conditions that she could not change. Her brain ached with contemplation of the cruel necessity that tortured humankind. Her very soul was sick with the hopelessness of the gasping, choking, struggling, multitude who, in their poverty and blindness, toiled to preserve their lives of sorrow and pain and sought relief from their labors in pleasures more horrible and destructive, by far, than the slavery to which they gave themselves for the means to pay.

The woman was tired--very tired. Heart and nerves and brain and soul and body were tired with a weariness that, it seemed to her, would never pass. She was tired of the life into which she had gone because it was the custom of the age and because of her necessity--the life into which she had not wished to go because it denied her womanhood. Because she knew herself to be a woman, she felt that she was being robbed of the things of her womanhood. The brightness and beauty, the strength and joyousness of her womanhood were, by her, held as sacred trusts to be kept for her children and, through them, for the race. She wearied of the struggle to keep the things of her womanhood from the world that was taking them from her--that put a price upon them--that used them as thoughtlessly as it uses the stone and metal and wood that it takes from the earth. She was tired of the horrid life that crowded her so closely--that crushed itself against her in the crowded cars--that leered into her face on the street--that reached out for her from every side--that hungered for her with a fierce hunger and longed for her with a damnable, fiendish, longing. She was faint and weak from contact with the loathsome things that she was forced to know and that would leave their mark upon her womanhood as surely as the touch of pitch defiles. And she was weary, so weary, waiting for that one with whom she could cross the threshold of the old, old, open door.

Little time was left to her, now, for thought and preparation for the life of which she had dreamed. Little heart was left to her, now, for dreaming. Little courage was left for hope. But still her dreams lived. Still she waited. Still, at times, she hoped.

But the thing that most of all wearied the woman, who knew that she was a woman, was this: the restless, discontented, dissatisfied, uneasy, spirit of the age that, scorning Tradition in a shallow, silly pride, struggles for and seems to value only that which is new regardless of the value of the thing itself. The new in dress, regardless of beauty or fitness in the costume--the new in thought, regardless of the saneness of the thinking--the new in customs and manner of living--the new in the home, in marriage relation, in the education and rearing of children--new philosophy, new science, new religion, new art, new music, new books, new cooking, new women--it sometimes appears that the crime of crimes, the most degrading disgrace, these days, is to be held old-fashioned, behind-the-times, out-of-date, and that everything, *everything*, not new is old-fashioned--everything not of the times is behind-the-times-- everything not down-to-date is out-of-date.

Patriotism, love of country, is old, very old, and is also--or therefore--quite out-of-date. To speak or write of patriotism, seriously, or to consider it a factor in life--to live it, depend upon it, or appeal to it, is to be considered very strange and sadly old-fashioned. The modern, down-to-date, age considers seriously not patriotism but "graft" and "price" and "boodle." These are the modern forces by which the nation is said to be governed; these are the means by which the nation strives to go ahead. To talk only of these things, to believe only in these things, to live only these things, is to be modern and down--low down--to-date. To work from any motive but the making of money is to be queerly behind-the-times. To write a book or paint a picture or sing a song, to preach a sermon, to do anything for any reason under heaven but for cash marks you a fanatic and a fool. To believe, even, that anyone does anything save for the money there is in it stamps you simple and unsophisticated, indeed. To profess such belief, save you put your tongue in your cheek, marks you peculiar.

Long, long, ago mankind put its best strength, its best thought, its best life, into its works, without regard for the price, simply because it was its work. And the work so wrought in those queer old-fashioned days has most curiously endured. There is little danger that much of our modern, down-to-date work will endure for the very simple reason that we do not want it to endure. "The world wants something new." Down-to-date-ism does not want its work to last longer than the dollar it brings. Never fear, the world is getting something new! But, though we have grown so bravely away from those queer, old-fashioned days we have not succeeded yet in growing altogether away from the works that those old-fashioned days produced. But, patience, old world--patience--down-to-date-ism may, in time, accomplish even this.

In those old, old, times, too, it was the fashion for men and women to mate in love. In love, they planned and built their homes. In love, they brought forth children and reared them, with queer, old-fashioned notions about marriage, to serve the race. In those times, now so sadly old and out-of-date, men planned and labored for homes and children and women were home makers and mothers. But the world is now far from those ancient ways and out-of-date ideals. Marriage has little to do with home making these modern days. It has almost nothing to do with children. We have, in our down-to-date-ism, come to be a nation of childless wives and homeless husbands. We are dwellers in flats, apartments, hotels, where children would be in the way but dogs are welcome if only they be useless dogs. We live in houses that are always for sale or rent. It is our proud boast that we possess nothing that is not on the market for a price. The thought of selling a home is not painful for we do not know, the value of a home. We have, for convenience, to gratify our modern, down-to-date, ever changing tastes, popularized the divorce court as though a husband or wife of more than three seasons is old-fashioned and should be discarded for one of a newer pattern, more in harmony with our modern ideals of marriage.

From the down-to-date--the all-the-way-down-to-date woman, I mean--one gains new and modern ideas of the service that womankind is to render to the race. Almost it is as though God did not know what he was about when he made woman. To place a home above a club; a nursery above the public platform; a fireside above politics; the prattle of children above newspaper notoriety; the love of boys and girls above the excitement of social conquest; the work of bearing strong men and true women for the glory of the race above the near intellectual pursuits and the attainments of a shallow thinking; all this is to be sadly old-fashioned. All this is so behind-the-times that one must confess such shocking taste with all humiliation.

I hereby beg pardon of the down-to-date powers that be, and most humbly pray that they will graciously forgive my boorishness. I assure you that, after all, I am not so benighted that I do not realize how seriously babies would interfere in the affairs of those down-to-date women who are elevating the race. By all means let the race be elevated though it perish, childless, in the process. Very soon, now, womanhood itself will be out-of-date for the world, in this also, seems to be evolving something new.

So the woman, who knew herself to be a woman, most of all, was tired of things new and longed, deep in her heart, for the old, old, things that were built into the very foundation of the race and that no amount of gilding and trimming and ornamenting can ever cover up or hide; and no amount of disregarding or ignoring can do away with; lest indeed the race perish from the earth.

"And when do you take your vacation?" asked a fellow worker as they were leaving the building after the day's work.

"Not until the last of the month," returned the woman wearily. "And you?"

"Me, oh, I must go Monday! And it's such a shame! I've just received a charming invitation for two weeks later but no one cares to exchange time with me. No one, you see, can go on such short notice. I don't suppose that you--" she paused suggestively.

"I will exchange time with you," said the woman simply.

"Will you really? Now, that *is* clever of you! Are you *sure* that you don't mind?"

"Indeed, I will be glad to get away earlier."

"But can you get ready to go so soon?"

The woman smiled. "I shall do very little getting ready."

The other looked at her musingly. "No, I suppose not, you are so queer that way. Seems to me I can't find time enough to make new things. One just *must* keep up, you know."

"It is settled then?" asked the woman, at the corner where they parted.

"It will be so good of you," murmured the other.

The woman had many invitations to spend her brief vacation with friends, but, that night, she wrote a letter to the people who lived in her old home and asked if they would take her for two weeks, requesting that they telegraph their answer. When the message came, she wired them to meet her and went by the first train.

At the old home station, her train took a siding at the upper end of the yards to let the outgoing express pass. From the window where she sat the woman saw a tall man, dressed in a business suit of quiet gray, standing on the rear platform of the slowly moving outbound train and waving his hand to someone on the depot platform. Just a glimpse she had of him before he passed from sight as her own train moved ahead to stop at the depot where she was greeted by her host. Not until they were driving toward her old home did the woman know who it was that she had seen.

The woman was interested in all that the people had to tell about her old playmate and asked not a few questions but she was glad that he had not known of her coming. She was glad that he was gone. The man and the woman were strangers and the woman did not wish to meet a stranger. The boy lived, for her, only in her Yesterdays and the woman told herself that she was glad because she feared that the man, if she met him, would rob her of the boy. She feared that he would be like so many that she had been forced to know in the world that denied her womanhood. She had determined to be for two weeks, as far as it is possible for a woman to be, just a girl again and she wanted no company other than the little boy who lived only in the long ago.

As soon as supper was over she retired to her room--to the little room that had been hers in her childhood--where, before lighting the lamp, she sat for awhile at the open window looking out into the night, breathing long and deep of the pure air that was sweetly perfumed with the odor of the meadows and fields. In the brooding quiet; in the soft night sounds; in the fragrant breeze that gently touched her hair; she felt the old, old, forces of life calling to her womanhood and felt her womanhood stir in answer. For a long time she sat there giving free rein to the thoughts and longings that, in her city life, she was forced to suppress.

Rising at last, as though with quick resolution, she lighted her lamp and prepared for bed; loosening her hair and deftly arranging the beautiful, shining, mass that fell over her shoulders in a long braid. Then, smiling as she would have smiled at the play of a child, she knelt before her trunk and, taking something from its depth, quickly put out the light again and once more seated herself in a low rocking chair by the open window.

Had there been any one to see, they would not have understood. Who is there, indeed, to understand the heart of womanhood? The woman, sitting in the dark before the window in that room so full of the memories of her childhood, held close in her arms an ancient doll whose face had been washed so many times by its little mother that it was but a smudge of paint.

That night the woman slept as a child sleeps after a long, busy, happy, childhood day--slept to open her eyes in the morning while the birds in the trees outside her window were heralding the coming of the sun. Rising she looked and saw the sky glorious with the light of dawning day. Flaming streamers of purple and scarlet and silver floated high over the buildings and trees next door. The last of the pale stars sank into the ocean of blue and, from behind the old orchard above the house where the boy lived, long shafts of golden light shot up as if aimed by some heavenly archer hiding behind the hill.

When the day was fully come, the woman quickly dressed and went out into the yard. The grass was dew drenched and fragrant under her feet. The flowers were fresh and inviting. But she did not pause until, out in the garden, at the farther corner, close by the hedge, she stood under the cherry tree--sacred cathedral of her Yesterdays.

When she turned again to go back to the house, the woman's face was shining with the light that glows only in the faces of those women who know that they are women and who dream the dreams of womanhood.

So the woman spent her days. Down in the little valley by the brook, that, as it ran over the pebbly bars, drifted in the flickering light and shade of the willows, slipped between the green banks, or crept softly beneath the grassy arch, sang its song of the Yesterdays: up in the orchard beyond the neighboring house where so many, many, times she had helped the boy play out his dreams; on the porch, in the soft twilight, watching the stars as they blossomed above while up from the dusky shadows in the valley below came the call of the whip-poor-will and the bats on silent wings flitted to and fro; out in the garden under the cherry tree in the corner near the hedge--in all the loved haunts of the boy and girl--she spent her days.

And the tired look went out of her eyes. Strength returned to her weary body, courage to her heart, and calmness to her overwrought nerves. Amid those scenes of her Yesterdays she was made ready to go back to the world that values so highly things that are new, and, in the strength of the old, old, things to keep the dreams of her womanhood. And, as she went, there was that in her face that all men love to see in the face of womankind.

Poor old world! Someday, perhaps, it will awake from its feverish dream to find that God made some things in the heart of the race too big to be outgrown.

TEMPTATION

The heights of Life are fortified. They are guarded by narrow passes where the world must go single file and where, if one slip from the trail, he falls into chasms of awful depths; by cliffs of apparent impassable abruptness which, if in scaling, one lose his head he is lost; and by false trails that seem to promise easy going but lead in the wrong direction. Not in careless ease are those higher levels gained. The upward climb is one of strenuous effort, of desperate struggle, of hazardous risk. Only those who prove themselves fit may gain the top.

Somewhere in the life of every man there is a testing time. There is a trial to prove of what metal he is made. There is a point which, won or lost, makes him winner or loser in the game. There is a Temptation that to him is vital.

To pray: "Lead us not into temptation," is divine wisdom for Temptation lies in wait. There is no need to seek it. And, when once it is met, there is no dodging the issue or shifting the burden of responsibility. In the greatest gifts that men possess are the seeds which, if grown and cultivated, yield poisonous fruit. In the very forces that men use for greatest good are the elements of their own destruction. And, whatever the guise in which Temptation comes, the tempter is always the same--Self. Temptation spells always the mastery of or the surrender to one's self.

Once I stood on a mighty cliff with the ocean at my feet. Ear below, the waves broke with a soothing murmur that scarce could reach my ears and the gray gulls were playing here and there like shadows of half forgotten dreams. In the distance, the fishing boats rolled lazily on the gentle swell and the sunlight danced upon the surface of the sea. Then, as I looked, on the far horizon the storm chieftain gathered his clans for war. I saw the red banners flashing. I watched the hurried movements of the dark and threatening ranks. I heard the rumbling tread of the tramping feet. And, like airy messengers sent to warn me, the gusts of wind came racing and wailed and sobbed about the cliff because I would not heed their warning. The startled boats in the offing spread their white wings and scurried to the shelter of their harbor nests. The gray gulls vanished. The sunlight danced no more upon the surface of the sea. And then, as the battle front rolled above my head, the billows, lashed to fury by the wind and flinging in the air the foam of their own madness, came rushing on to try their strength against the grim and silent rock. Again and again they hurled their giant forms upon the cliff, until the roar of the surf below drowned even the thunder in the clouds above and the solid earth trembled with the shock, but their very strength was their ruin and they were dashed in impotent spray from the stalwart object of their assault. And at last, when the hours of the struggle were over; when the storm soldiers had marched on to their haunts behind the hills; when the gulls had returned to their sports; and the sun shone again on the waters; I saw the bosom of the ocean rise and fall like the breast of an angry child exhausted with its passion while the cliff, standing stern and silent, seemed to look, with mingled pride and pity, upon its foe now moaning at its feet.

Like that cliff, I say, is the soul of a man who, in temptation, gains the mastery of himself. The storm clouds of life may gather darkly over his head but he shall not tremble. The lightning of the world's wrath and the thunder of man's disapproval shall not move him. The waves of passion that so try the strength of men shall be dashed in impotent spray from his stalwart might. And when, at last, the storms of life are over--when the sun shines again on the waters as it shone before the fight began--he shall still stand, calm and unmoved, master of himself and men.

Because those things are true, I say: that Temptation is one of the Thirteen Truly Great Things of Life.

And the man knew these things--knew them as well as you know them. In the full knowledge of these things he came to his testing time. To win or to lose, in the full knowledge of all that victory or defeat meant to him, he went to his Temptation.

It was early winter when his time came but he knew that first morning after he had returned from his vacation that it was coming. The moment he entered the room to take up again the task of putting his dreams into action, he saw her and felt her power for she was one of those women who compel recognition of their sex as the full noonday sun compels recognition of its light and heat.

An hour later her duties brought her to him, and, for a few moments, they stood face to face. And the man, while he instructed her in the work that she was to do, felt the strength of her power even as a strong swimmer feels the current of the stream. Through her eyes, in her voice, in her presence, this woman challenged the man, made him more conscious of her than of his work. The subtle, insinuating, luring, strength of her beat upon him, enveloped him, thrilled him. As she turned to go back to her place, his eyes followed her and he knew that he was approaching a great crisis in his life. He knew that soon or late he would be forced into a battle with himself and that tremendous stakes would be at issue. He knew that victory would give him increased power, larger capacity, and a firmer grip upon the enduring principles of life or defeat would make of him a slave, with enfeebled spirit, humiliated and ashamed.

Every day, in the weeks that followed, the man was forced to see her--to talk with her--to feel her strength. And every day he felt himself carried irresistibly onward toward the testing that he knew must come. He was conscious, too, that the woman, also, knew and understood and that it pleased her so to use her power. She willed that he should feel her presence. In a thousand subtle forms she repeated her challenge. In ways varied without number she called to him, lured him, led him. To do this seemed a necessity to her. She was one of those women whose natures seem to demand this expression of themselves. Instinctively, she made all men with whom she came in contact feel her power and, instinctively--unconsciously, perhaps--she gloried in her strength.

If the man could have had other things in common with her it would have been different. If there had been, as well, the appeal of the intellect--of the spirit--if the beauty of her had been to him an expression of something more than her sex--if there had been ideals, hopes, longings, fears, even sorrow or regret, common to both, it would have been different. But there was nothing. Often the man sought to find something more but there was nothing. So he permitted himself to be carried onward by a current against which, when the time should come, he knew he would need to fight with all his might. And always, as the current swept him onward toward the point where he must make the decisive struggle, he felt the woman's power over him growing ever greater.

At last it came.

It was Saturday. The man left the place where he worked earlier than usual that he might walk to his rooms for he felt the need of physical action. He felt a strong desire to run, to leap, to use his splendid muscles that throbbed and exulted with such vigorous life. As he strode along the streets, beyond the business district, he held his head high, he looked full into the faces of the people he met with a bold challenging look. The cool, bracing air, of early winter was grateful on his glowing skin and he drank long deep breaths of it as one would drink an invigorating tonic. Every nerve and fiber of him was keenly, gloriously, alive with the strength of his splendid manhood. Every nerve and fiber of him was conscious of her and exulted in that which he had seen in her eyes when she had told him that she would be at home that evening and that she would be glad to have him call. With all his senses abnormally alert, he saw and noted everything about him. A thousand trivial, commonly unseen things, along his way and in the faces, dress, and manner, of the people whom he met, caught his eye. Yet, always, vividly before him, was the face of her whose power he had felt. Under it all, he was conscious that this was his testing time. He *knew*--or it would have been no Temptation--it would have been no trial. Impatiently he glanced at his watch and, as he neared the place where he lived, quickened his stride, springing up the steps of the house at last with a burst of eager haste.

In the front hall, at the foot of the stairs, the little daughter of his landlady greeted him with shouts of delight and, with the masterful strength of four feminine years, dragged him, a willing captive, through the open door to her mother's pleasant sitting room. She was a beautiful, dainty, little miss with hair and eyes very like that playmate of the man's Yesterdays and it was his custom to pay tribute to her charms in the coin of childhood as faithfully and as regularly as he paid his board.

Seated now, with the baby on his lap and the smiling mother

looking on, he produced, after the usual pretense of denial and long search through many pockets, the weekly offering. And then, as though some guardian angel willed it so, the little girl did a thing that she had never done before. Putting two plump and dimpled arms about his neck she said gravely: "Mamma don't like me to kiss folks, you know, but she said she wouldn't care if I kissed *you*" Whereupon a sweet little rosebud mouth was offered trustingly, with loving innocence, to his lips.

A crimson flame flushed the man's face. With a laugh of embarrassment and a quick impulsive hug he held the child close and accepted her offering.

Then he went quickly upstairs to his room.

It was sometime later when the man began to prepare for the evening to which he had looked forward with such eagerness and all his fierce and driving haste was gone. The mad tumult of his manhood strength was stilled. He moved, now, with a purpose, sullen, grim, defiant. The fight was on. While he was still vividly conscious of the woman whose compelling power he felt, he felt, now, as well, the pure touch of those baby lips. While he still saw the light in the woman's eyes and sensed the meaning of her smile, he saw and sensed as clearly the loving innocence that had shown in the little girl's face as it was lifted up to his. Upon his manhood's strength lay the woman's luring spell. Upon his manhood the baby's kiss lay as a seal of sacredness--upon his lips it burned as a coal of holy fire. The fight was on.

The man's life was not at all an easy life. Beside his work and his memories there was little to hold him true. Since that day when he stood face to face with Life and, for the first time, knew that he was a man, he had been, save for a few friends among the men of his own class, alone. The exacting demands of his work had left him little time or means to spend in seeking social pleasures or in the delights of fellowship with those for whose fellowship he would have cared, even had the way to their society been, at that period of his life, open to him. He told himself, always, that sometime in the future, when he had worked out still farther his dreams, he would find the way to the social life that he would enjoy but until then, he must, of necessity, live much alone. And now--now--the testing time--the crisis in his life--had come. Even as it must come to every man who knows his manhood so it had come to him.

The man was not deceived. He knew the price he would pay in defeat. But, even while he knew this--even while he knew what defeat would mean to him, so great was her power that he went on making ready to go to her. With the kiss of the little girl upon his lips he made ready to go to the woman. It was as though he had drifted too far and the current had become too strong for him to turn back. Thus do such men yield to such temptations. Thus are men betrayed by the very strength of their manhood.

With mad determination he waited the hour. Uneasily he paced his room. He tried to read. He threw himself into a chair only to arise and move about again. Every few moments he impatiently consulted his watch. At every step in the hall, without his door, he started as if alarmed. He became angry, in a blind rage, with the woman, with himself and even with the little girl. At last, when it was time to go, he threw on his overcoat, took his hat and gloves, and, with a long, careful look about the room, laid his hand on the door. He knew that the man who was going out that evening would not come hack to his room the same man. He knew that *that* man could never come back. He felt as though he was giving up his apartments to a stranger. So he hesitated, with his hand upon the door, looking long and carefully about. Then quickly he threw open the door and, down the hall and down the stairs, went as one who has counted the cost and determined recklessly.

The man had opened the front door and was about to pass out when a sweet voice called: "Wait, oh, wait."

Turning, he saw a tiny figure in white flying toward him.

The little girl, all ready for bed, had caught sight of him and, for the moment, had escaped from her mother's attention.

The man shut the door and caught her up. Two dimpled arms went around his neck and the rosebud mouth was lifted to his lips.

Then the mother came and led her away while the man stood watching her as she went.

Would he ever dare touch those baby lips again he wondered. Could he, he asked himself, could he face again those baby eyes? Could he ever again bear the feeling of that soft little body in his arms?

At the farther end of the hall, she turned, and, seeing him still there, waved her hand with a merry call: "Good-bye, good-bye."

Then she passed from his sight and, in place of this little girl of rosy, dimpled, flesh, the startled man saw a dainty maiden of his Yesterdays, standing under a cherry tree with fallen petals of the delicate blossoms in her wayward hair, and with eyes that looked at him very gravely and a little frightened as, for the shaggy coated minister, he spoke the solemn words: "I pronounce you husband and wife and anything that God has done must never be done any different by anybody forever and ever, Amen." By some holy magic the kiss of the little girl became the kiss of his play wedding wife of the long ago.

Very slowly the man went up the stairs again to his room; there to spend the evening not as he had planned, when he was in the mastering grip of self, but safe in the quiet harbor of the Yesterdays where the storms of life break not or are felt only in those gentle ripples that scarce can stir the surface of the sea.

The fierce passion that had shaken the very soul of him passed on as the storm clouds pass. In the calm of the days that were gone, he rested as one who has fought a good fight and, safe from out the turmoil and the danger, has come victoriously into the peace that passeth all understanding.

In the sweet companionship of his childhood mate, with the little girl who lived next door, the man found again, that night, his better self. In the boy of the long-ago, he found again his ideals of manhood. In his Yesterdays, he found strength to stand against the power of the temptation that assailed him.

Blessed, blessed Yesterdays!

* * * * *

It was the time of the first snow when, again, the woman sat alone in her room before the fire, with her door fast locked and the shades drawn close, even as on that other night--the night when her womanhood began in dreams.

In the soft dusk, while the shadows of the flickering light came and went upon the walls, and the quiet was broken only by the tick, tick, tick, of the timepiece held in the chubby arms of the fat cupid on the mantle, the woman sat very still. Face to face with her Temptation, she sat alone and very still.

For several months, the woman had seen her testing time approaching. That day when, looking into her eyes, the man of authority had so kindly bidden her leave her work for the afternoon, she had known that this time would come. In the passing weeks she had realized that the day was approaching when she must decide both for him and for herself. She had not sought to prevent the coming of that day. She had knowingly permitted it to come. She was even pleased in a way to watch it drawing near. Not once, in those weeks, had he failed to be very kind or ceased to make her feel that he understood. In a hundred ways, as their work called them together and gave opportunity, he had told her, in voice and look and the many ways of wordless speech, that the time was coming. He had been very careful, too--very careful--that, in their growing friendship, the world should have no opportunity to misjudge. And the woman, seeing his care, was grateful and valued his friendship the more.

So had come at last that Saturday when, with low spoken words, at the close of the day's work, he had asked if he might call upon her the following evening; saying gravely, as he looked down into her face, that he had something very important to tell her. And she had gravely said that he might come; while her blushes to him confessed that she knew what it was of importance that he would say.

Scarcely had she reached her home that afternoon when a messenger boy appeared with a great armful of roses and, as she arranged the flowers on her table, burying her flushed face again and again in their fragrant coolness, she had told herself that to-morrow, when he asked her to cross with him the threshold of that old, old door, she would answer: yes. But, even as she so resolved, she had been conscious of something in her heart that denied the resolution of her mind.

And so it was that, as she sat alone before her fire that night, she knew that she was face to face with a crisis in her life. So it was that she had come to the testing time and knew that she must win or lose alone. In the sacred privacy of her room, with the perfume of his roses filling the air and the certainty that when he came on the morrow she must answer, she looked into the future to see, if she might, what it held for her and for him if she should cross with him the threshold of that old, old, door.

He was a man whose love would honor any woman--this she knew. And he was a man of power and influence in the world--a man who could provide for his mate a home of which any woman would be proud to be the mistress. Nor could she doubt his love for nothing else could have persuaded such a man to ask of a woman that which he was coming to ask of her.

Beginning with her answer on the following evening the woman traced, in thought, all that would follow. She saw herself leaving the life that she had never desired because it could not recognize her womanhood and, in fancy, received the congratulations of her friends. She lived, in her imagination, those busy days when she would be making ready for the day that was to come. Very clearly, she pictured to herself the wedding; it would be a quiet wedding, she told herself, but as beautiful and complete as cultured taste and wealth could make it. Then they would go away, for a time, to those cities and lands beyond the sea that, all her life, she had longed to visit. When they returned, it would be to that beautiful old home of his family--the home that she had so often, in passing, admired; and in that home, so long occupied by him alone, she would be the proud mistress. And then--then--would come her children--their children--and so all the fulfillment of her womanhood's dreams.

But the woman's face, as she looked into a future that seemed as bright as ever woman dared to dream, was troubled. As she traced the way that lay so invitingly before her, this woman, who knew herself to be a woman, was sad. Her heart, still, was as an empty room--a room that is furnished and ready but without a tenant. Deep within her woman heart she knew that this man was not the one for whom she waited by the open door. She did not know who it was for whom she waited. She knew only that this man was not the one. And she wished--oh, how she wished--that this was not so. Because of her longing--because of the dreams of her womanhood--because of her empty heart--she was resolved to cross with this man, who was not the man for whom she waited, the threshold that she could not cross alone. Honor, regard, respect, the affection of a friend, she could give him--did give him indeed--but she knew that this was not enough for a woman to give the man with whom she would enter that old, old, door.

Rising, the woman went to her mirror to study long and carefully the face and form that she saw reflected there. She saw in the glass, a sweet, womanly, beauty, expressing itself in the color and tone of the clean carved features; in the dainty texture of the clear skin and soft, brown, hair; and in the rounded fullness and graceful lines of the finely moulded body. Perfect physical strength and health was there--vital, glowing, appealing. And culture of mind, trained intelligence, thoughtfulness, was written in that womanly face. And, with it all, there was good breeding, proud blood, with gentleness of spirit.

This woman knew that she was well equipped to stand by this man's side however high his place in life. She was well fitted to become the mistress of his home and the mother of his children. She had guarded well the choicest treasures of her womanhood. She had squandered none of the wealth that was committed to her. She had held it all as a sacred trust to be kept by her for that one with whom she should go through the old, old door. And she had determined that, to-morrow evening, she would give herself, with all the riches of her womanhood, to this one who could give her, in return, the home of her dreams. While her heart was still as an empty room, she had determined to cross, with this man, the threshold over which no woman may again return.

Turning from her mirror, slowly the woman went to the great bunch of roses that stood upon her table. They were his roses; and they fitly expressed, in their costly beauty, the life that he was coming to offer to her. Very deliberately she bent over them, burying her face in the mass of rich color, inhaling deeply their heavy fragrance. Thoughtfully she considered them and all that, to her, they symbolized. But there was no flush upon her cheek now. There was no warmth in the light of her eyes. No glad excitement thrilled her. There was no trembling in her touch--no eager joyousness in her manner.

Suddenly, some roisterer, passing along the street with his companions, laughed a loud, reckless, half drunken, laugh that sounded in the quiet darkness with startling clearness.

The woman sprang back from the flowers as though a poisonous serpent, hidden in their fragrant beauty, had struck her. With a swift look of horror on her white face she glanced fearfully about the room.

Again the laugh sounded; this time farther down the street.

The woman sank into her chair, trembling with a nameless fear. To her, that laugh in the dark had sounded as the laughter of the crowd that day when she was forced so close to the outcast women who were in the hands of the police.

"But those women," argued the frightened woman with herself, "sell themselves to all men for a price."

"And you," answered the heart of her womanhood, "and you, also, will sell yourself to one man, for a price. The wealth of womanhood committed to you--all the treasures that you have guarded so carefully--you will sell now to this good man for the price that he can pay. If he could not pay the price--if he came to you empty handed--would you say yes?"

"But I will be true to him," argued the woman. "I will give myself to him and to him only as wife to husband."

"You are being false to him already," replied her woman heart, "for you are selling yourself, not giving yourself to him. You are planning to deceive him. You would make him think that he is taking to himself a wife when, for a price, you are selling to him--something higher than a public woman, it is true--but something, as true, very much lower than a wife. What matter whether the price be in gold and silver or in property and social position--it is a price. Except he pay you your price he could not have you."

And what, thought the woman, what if--after she had crossed the threshold with this good man--after she had entered with him into the life that lay on the other side that door--what if, then, that other one should come? What if the one for whom her empty heart should have waited were to come and stand alone before that door through which she could not go back? And the children--the dear children of her dreams--what of them? Had not her unborn children the right to demand that they be born in love? And if she should say, "no," to this man--if she should turn once more away from the open door, through which he would ask her to go with him--what then? What if that one who had delayed his coming so long should never come?

And then the woman, who knew herself to be a woman, saw the lonely years come and go. While she waited without the door that led to the life of her womanhood's dreams, she saw the beauty that her mirror revealed slowly fading--saw her firm, smooth, cheeks become thin and wrinkled, her bright eyes grow dim and pale, her soft, brown, hair turn thin and gray, her body grow lean and stooped. All the wealth of her womanhood that she had treasured with such care she saw become as dust, worthless. All the things of her womanhood she would be forced to spend in that life that denied her womanhood, and then, when she had nothing left, she would be cast aside as a worn out machine. Never to know the joy of using her womanhood! Never to have a home! Never to feel the touch of a baby hand! To lay down the wealth of her woman life and go empty and alone in her shriveled old age! With an exclamation, the woman sprang to her feet and stretched out her arms. "No, no, no," she whispered fiercely, "anything, anything, but that. I will be true to him. I will be a faithful wife. He shall never know. He shall not feel that he is cheated. And perhaps--" she dropped into her chair again and buried her face in her hands as she whispered--"perhaps, bye and bye, God will let me love him. Surely, God will let me love him, bye and bye."

Sometime later, the woman did a strange thing. Going to her desk, softly, as a thief might go, she unlocked a drawer and took from it a small jewel case. For several moments she stood under the light holding the little velvet box in her hand unopened. Then, lifting the lid, she looked within and, presently, from among a small collection of trinkets that had no value save to her who knew their history, took a tiny brass ring. Placing the box on the dresser, she tried, musingly, to fit the little ring on her finger. On each finger in turn she tried, but it would go only part way on the smallest one; and she smiled sadly to see how she had grown since that day under the cherry tree.

Turning again, she went slowly across the room to the fire that now was a bed of glowing coals. For a little she stood looking down into the fire. Then, slowly, she stretched forth her hand to drop the ring. But she could not do it. She could not.

Returning the little circle of brass to its place among the trinkets in the jewel box, the woman prepared for bed.

The timepiece in the arms of the fat cupid ticked loudly now in the darkness that was only faintly relieved by the glowing embers of the fire.

With sleepless eyes the woman who had determined to give herself without love lay staring into the dusk. But she did not see the darkness. She did not see the grotesque and ghostly objects in the gloom. Nor did she see the somber shadows that came and went as the dying fire gained fitful strength. The woman saw the bright sun shining on the meadows and fields of the long ago. She saw again the scenes of her childhood. Again, as she stood under the cherry tree that showered its delicate blossoms down with every puff of air, she looked with loving confidence into the face of the brown cheeked boy who spoke so seriously those childish vows. Again, upon her lips she felt that kiss of the childhood mating.

The soft light of the fire grew fainter and fainter as the embers slowly turned to ashes. Could it be that the woman, in her temptation, would let the sacred fire of love burn altogether out? Must the memories of her Yesterdays turn to ashes too?

The last faint glow was almost gone when the woman slipped quickly out of her bed and, in the darkness, groped her way across the room to the desk where she found the little jewel case.

And I think that the fat cupid who was neglecting his bow and arrows to wrestle with time must have been pleased to see the woman, a little later, when the dying fire flared out brightly for a moment, lying fast asleep, while, upon the little finger of the hand that lay close to her smiling lips, there was a tiny circle of brass.

LIFE

IN childhood, the Master of Life exalts Life. A baby in its mother's arms is the fullest expression of Divinity.

It was Christmas time; that season of the year when, for a brief period, the world permits the children to occupy the place in the affairs and thoughts of men that is theirs by divine right.

In the birth of that babe in Bethlehem, the Giver of Life placed the seal of his highest approval upon childhood and decreed that, until the end of time, babies should be the true rulers of mankind and the lawful heirs of heaven. And it is so, that the power of Mary's babe, from his manger cradle throne, has been more potent on earth in the governments of men than the strength of many emperors with their armed hosts.

It is written large in Nature's laws that mankind should be governed by love of children. The ruling purpose and passion of the race can be, with safety, nothing less than the purpose and passion of all created things--of even the trees and plants--the purpose to reproduce its kind--the passion for its offspring. The world should be ruled by boys and girls.

But Mammon has usurped the throne of Life. His hosts have trampled the banners of loyal love in the dust. His forces have compelled the rightful rulers of the world to abdicate. But, even as gross materialism has never succeeded in altogether denying Divinity, so, for a few days each year, at Christmas time, childhood asserts its claims and compels mankind to render, at least a show, of homage.

Poor, blind, deceived and betrayed, old world; to so fear a foolish and impotent anarchism that spends its strength in vain railings against governments while you pay highest honors and present your choicest favors to those traitors who filch your wealth of young life under pretense of loyal service. The real anarchists, old world, are not those who loudly vociferate to the rabble on the street corners but those who, operating under the laws of your approval, betray their country in its greatest need--its need of children. The real anarchists, old world, are those whose banners are made red by the blood of babies; who fatten upon the labor of their child slaves; and who seek to rule by the slaughter of children even as that savage of old whose name in history is hated by every lover of the race. Regicides at heart, they are, for they kill, for a price, the God ordained rulers of mankind. A child is nearer, by many years, to God than the grown up rebel who traitorously holds his own mean interests superior to the holy will of Life as vested in the sacred person of a boy or girl.

To prate, in empty swelling words, of the sacredness of life, the power of religion, the dignity of state, the importance of commercial interests and the natural wealth of the nation, while ignoring the sacredness, power, dignity, importance, and wealth of childhood, is evidence of a criminal thoughtlessness.

Children and Life are one. They are the product, the producers, and the preservers of Life. They exalt Life. They interpret

Life. Without them Life has no meaning. The child is no more the possession of its parents than the parents are the property of the child. Children are the just creditors of the human race. Mankind owes them everything. They owe mankind nothing. A baby has no debts.

Nor is the passion for children satisfied only in bearing them. A woman who does not love *all* babies is unsafe to trust with one of her own flesh. A man who does not love *all* children is unfit to father offspring of his own blood. One need not die to orphan a child. One need only refuse to care for it. One need only place other interests first. Men and women who desire to become parents will not go unsatisfied in a world that is so full of boys and girls for whom there are neither fathers nor mothers.

The Master of Life said: "Except ye become as little children." His false disciple--world--teaches: "Except ye become grown up." But the laws of Life are irrevocable. If a man, heeding the world, grows up to possess the earth, his holdings, at the last, are reduced--if he be one of earth's big men--to six feet of it, only; while the man who never grows up inherits a heaven that the false kings of earth know not.

When the man left his work, at close of the day before Christmas, he was as eager as he had been that Saturday when he faced the crisis of his life. With every sense keenly alive, he plunged into the throng of belated shoppers that filled the streets and crowded into the gaily decked stores until it overflowed into the streets again. Nearly everyone was carrying bundles and packages for it was too late, now, to depend upon the overworked delivery wagons. In almost every face, the Christmas gladness shone. In nearly every voice, there was that spirit of fellowship and cheery good will that is invoked by Christmas thoughts and plans. Through the struggling but good natured crowd, the man worked his way into a store and, when he forced his way out again, his arms, too, were full. For a moment he waited on the corner for a car then, with a look of smiling dismay at the number of people who were also waiting, he turned away, determined to walk. He felt, too, that the exercise in the keen air would be a relief to the buoyant strength and gladness that clamored for expression.

As he swung so easily along the snowy pavement, with the strength of his splendid manhood revealed in every movement and the cleanness of his heart and mind illuminating his countenance, there were many among those he met who, while they smiled in sympathy with his spirit, passed from their smiles to half sighs of envy and regret.

With the impatient haste of a boy, the man dashed up the steps of his boarding house and ran up stairs to his room; chuckling in triumph over his escape from the watchful eyes of the little daughter of the house. For the first time since his boyhood the man was to have the blessed privilege of sharing the Christmas cheer of a home.

When the evening meal was over and it was time for his little playmate to go to sleep, he retired again to his room, almost as excited, in his eager impatience for the morning, as the child herself. Safe behind his closed door, he began to unwrap his Christmas packages and parcels that he might inspect again his purchases and taste, by anticipation, the pleasure he would know when on the morrow the child would discover his gifts. Very carefully he cut the strings from the last and largest package and, tenderly removing the wrappings, revealed a doll almost as tall as the little girl herself. It was as large, at least, as a real flesh and blood baby.

The wifeless, homeless, man who has never purchased a doll for some little child mother has missed an educational experience of more value than many of the things that are put in text books to make men wise.

Rather awkwardly the man held the big doll in his arms, smoothing its dress and watching the eyes that opened and closed so lifelike; cautiously he felt for and found that vital spot which if pressed brought forth a startling: "papa--mama."

As the dear familiar words of childhood sounded in the lonely bachelor room, the man felt a queer something grip his heart. Tenderly he laid the doll upon his big bed and stood for a little looking down upon it; a half-serious, half-whimsical, expression on his face but in his eyes a tender light. Then, adjusting his reading lamp, he seated himself and attempted to busy his strangely disturbed mind with a book. But the sentences were meaningless. At every period, his eyes turned to that little figure on the bed, with its too lifelike face and hair and form while the thoughts of the author he was trying to read were crowded out by other thoughts that forced themselves upon him with a persistency and strength that would not be denied.

The weeks following the testing of the man had been to him very wonderful weeks. He seemed to be living in a new world, or, rather, for him, the same old world was wonderfully enriched and glorified. Never had he felt his manhood's strength stirring so within him. Never had his mind been so alert, his spirit so bold. He moved among men with a new power that was felt by all who came in touch with him; though no one knew what it was. He was conscious of a fuller mastery of his work; a clearer grasp of the world events. As one, climbing in the mountains, reaches a point higher than he has ever before attained and gains thus a wider view of the path he has traveled, of the surrounding country, and of the peak that is the object of his climb as well, so this man, in his life climb, had reached a higher point and therefore gained a wider outlook. It is only when men stay in the lowlands of self interest or abide in the swamps of self indulgence that their views of life are narrowly circumscribed. Let a man master himself but once and he stands on higher ground, with wider outlook, with keener vision, and clearer atmosphere.

The man had always seen Life in its relation to himself; he came, now, to consider his own life in its relation to all Life; which point of view has all the difference that lies between a low valley and the mountain peaks that shut it in. He felt his relation, too, not alone to all human life but to all created things. With everything that lived he felt himself kin. With the very dray horses on the street, dragging with patient courage their heavily loaded trucks; with the stray dog that dodged in and out among the wheels and hoofs of the crowded traffic; even with the sparrow that perched for a moment on the ledge outside the window near his desk, he felt a kinship that was new and strange. Had they not all, he reflected, horse and dog and sparrow and man--had they not all one thing in common--Life? Was not Life the one thing supreme to each? Were they not, each one, a part of the whole? Was not the supreme object of every life, of all life, to live? Is the life of a man, he asked himself, more mysterious than the life of a horse? Can science--blind, pretentious, childish science--explain the life of a dog with less uncertainty than it can explain the life of a man? Or can the scientist make a laboratory sparrow more easily than he can produce a laboratory man? With the very trees that lined the streets near where he lived, he felt a kinship for they, too, within their trunks and limbs, had life--they, too, were parts of the whole even as he was a part--they, too, belonged even as he belonged.

Thus the man saw Life from a loftier height than he had ever before attained. Thus he sensed, as never before, the bigness, the fullness, the grandness, the awfulness, of Life. And so the man became very humble with a proud humbleness. He became very proud with a humble pride. He became even as a child again.

And then, standing thus upon this new height that he had gained, the man looked back into the ages that were gone and forward into the ages that were to come and so saw himself and his age a link between the past and the future; linking that which had been to that which was to be. All that Life had ever been-- the sum of all since the unknown beginning--was in the present. In the present, also, was all that Life could ever be, even unto the unknown end. Within his age and within himself he felt stirring all the mighty forces that, since the beginning, had wrought in the making of man. Within his age and within himself he felt the forces that would work out in the race results as far beyond his present vision as his age was beyond the ages of the most distant past.

Since the day when he had first realized his manhood, the working out of his dreams had been to the man the supreme object of his life. He had put his life, literally, into his work. For his work he had lived. But that Christmas eve, when his mind and heart were so filled with thoughts of childhood and those new emotions were aroused within him, he saw that the supreme thing in his life must be Life itself. He saw that not by putting his life into his work, would he most truly live, but by making his work contribute to his life. He realized that the greatest achievements of man are but factors in Life--that the one supreme, dominant, compelling, purpose of Life is to *live*--to *live*--to *live*--to express itself in Life--that the only adequate expression of Life *is* Life--that the passion of Life is to pass itself on--from age to age, from generation to generation, in a thousand thousand forms, in a thousand thousand ages, in a thousand thousand peoples, Life had passed itself on--was even then passing itself on--seeking ever fuller expression of itself; seeking ever to perfect itself; seeking ever to produce itself. He saw that the things that men do come out of their lives even as the plants come out of the soil into which the seed is dropped; and, that, even as the dead and decaying plant goes back into the earth from which it came, to enrich and renew the ground, so man's work, that comes out of his life, is reabsorbed again into his life to enrich and renew it. He realized, now, that the object of his life must be not his work but Life itself--that his effort must be not to do but to be--that he must accomplish not a great work but a great Life.

It was inevitable that the man should come to see, also, that the supreme glory of his manhood's strength was in this: the reproduction of his kind. The man life that ran so strongly in his veins, that throbbed so exultantly in his splendid body, that thrilled so keenly in his nerves--the man life that he had from his parents and from countless generations before--the life that made him kin to all his race and to all created things--this life he must pass on. This was the supreme glory of his manhood: that he could pass it on--that he could give it to the ages that were to come.

From the heights which he attained that Christmas eve, the man laughed at the empty, swelling, words of those who talk about the sacredness of work--who prattle as children about leaving a great work when they are gone--who gibber as fools about contributing a great work to the world.

If the men of a race will perfect the manhood strength of the race; if they will exalt their manhood power; if they will fulfill the mission of life by perfecting and producing ever more perfect lives; if they will endeavor to contribute to the ages to come stronger, better, men than themselves; why, the work of the world will be done--even as the plant produces its flowers and fruit, the work of the world will be done. In the exaltation of Life is the remedy for the evils that threaten the race. The reformations that men are always attempting in the social, religious, political, and industrial world are but attempts to change the flavor or quality of the fruit when it is ripening on the tree. The true remedy lies in the life of the tree; in the soil from which it springs; in the source from which the fruit derives its quality and flavor. In the appreciation of Life, in the passion of Life, in the production of Life, in the perfection of Life, in the exaltation of Life, is the salvation of human kind. For this, and this alone, man has right to live--has right to his place and part in Life.

All this the man saw that Christmas eve because the kiss of the little girl, on that night of his temptation, had awakened something in his manhood that was greater than the dreams he had been denying himself to work out. The friendship of the child had revealed to him this deeper truth of Life; that there are, for all true men, accomplishments greater than the rewards of labor. The baby had taught him that the legitimate fruit of love is more precious to Life, by far, than the wealth and honors that the world bestows--that, indeed, the greatest wealth, the highest honors, are not in the power of the world to give; nor are they to be won by toil. In his thinking, this man, too, was led by a little child.

The man's thoughts were interrupted by a knock at his door.

It was the little girl's mother; to tell him, as she had promised, that the child was safely asleep.

With his arms filled with presents, the man went softly down the stairs.

When all had been arranged for the morning, the man returned again to his room; but not to sleep. There was in his heart a feeling of reverent pride and gladness, as though he had been permitted to assist in a religious rite, and, with his own hands, to place an offering upon a sacred altar. And, if you will understand me, the man was right. Whatever else Christmas has come to mean to the grown up world, its true meaning can be nothing less than this.

Nor did the man again turn to his book or attempt to take up the train of thought that had so interfered with his reading. Something more compelling than any printed page--something more insistent than his own thoughts of Life and its meaning--lured him far away from his grown up days--took him back again into his days that were gone. Alone in his room that Christmas eve, the man went back, once more, to his Yesterdays--back to a Christmas in his Yesterdays.

Once again, his boyhood home was the scene of busy preparations for the Christmas gaieties. Once again, the boy, tucked snugly under the buffalo robe, drove with his parents away through the white fields to the distant town while the music in his heart kept time to the melody of the jingling bells. Once again, he experienced the happy perplexity of selecting--with mother's help--a present for father while father obligingly went to see a man on business and of choosing--with father's assistance--a gift for mother while she rested in a far corner of the store. And then, once again, he faced the trying question: what should he get for the little girl who lived next door. What, indeed, *could he get for her* but a beautiful new doll--one with brown hair, very like the little girl's own, and brown eyes that opened and closed as natural as life.

The next day the boy went, with his father and the little girl and her uncle, in the big sleigh, to the woods to find a tree for the Christmas "exercises" at the church; and, in the afternoon, in company with the older people, helped to make the wreaths of evergreen and deck the tree with glittering tinsel; while the little girl strung long strings of snowy pop corn and labored earnestly at the sweet task of filling mosquito bar stockings with candy and nuts.

Then came that triumphant Christmas eve, when, before the assembled Sunday school and the crowded church, the boy took part, with his class, in the entertainment and sat, with wildly beating heart, while the little girl, all alone, sang a Christmas carol; and proud he was, indeed, when the applause for the little singer was so long and loud. And then, when the farmer Santa Claus had distributed the last stocking of candy, the boy and the girl, with their elders, went home together, in the clear light of the stars;

while, across the white fields, came the sound of gay laughter and happy voices mingled with the ringing music of the sleigh bells--growing fainter and fainter--as friends and neighbors went their several ways.

But, best of all--by far the best of all--was that Christmas morning at home. At the first hint of gray light in the winter sky, the boy was awake and out of bed to gather his Christmas harvest; hailing each toy and game and book with exclamations of delight and arousing all the house with his shouts of: "Merry Christmas."

The foolish, grown up, old world has a saying that we value most the things that we win for ourselves by toil and hardship; but, believe me, it is not so. The real treasures of earth are the things that are won by the toil of those who bring to us, without price, the fruits of their labor as tokens of their love.

Very early, that long ago Christmas morning, the boy went over to the little girl's house; for his happiness would not be complete until he could share it with her. And the man, who, alone in his bachelor room that Christmas eve, dreamed of his Yesterdays, saw again, with startling clearness, his boyhood mate as she stood in the doorway greeting him with shouts of, "Merry Christmas," as he went toward her through the snow; and the heart of the man beat quicker at the lovely vision--even as the heart of the boy--for she held, close in her little mother arms, the new addition to her family of dolls--his gift. The lonely man, that night, realized, as he had never realized before, how full, at that moment, was the cup of the boy's proud happiness. He realized and understood.

I wonder--do you, also, understand?

In the still house, the big clock in the lower hall struck the hour. The man in his lonely room listened, counting the strokes --nine--ten--eleven--twelve.

It was Christmas.

* * * * *

And the woman, also, when she had passed safely through her trial, looked out upon Life from a point higher than she had ever reached before. Never before had Life, to her, looked so wide.

But the woman did not feel stronger after the crisis through which she had passed; she felt, more keenly than before, her weakness. More than ever, she felt the need of a strength that she could not find within herself. More than ever, she was afraid of the Life, that, from where she now stood, seemed so wide. Nor did she feel a kinship with all Life. She stood on higher ground, indeed, but the wideness of the view, to her, only emphasized her loneliness. She sadly felt herself as one apart--as one denied the right of fellowship. More keenly than ever before, she felt, in the heart of her womanhood, the humiliation of the life that sets a price upon the things of womanhood while it refuses to recognize womanhood itself. More than ever, in her woman heart, she was ashamed. Neither could she feel that she was doing her part in Life--that she was taking her place--that she was a link joining the ages of the past to the ages that would come. She felt herself, rather, a parasite, attached to Life--not a part of--not belonging to--but feeding upon.

This woman who knew herself to be a woman saw, more clearly than ever before, that one thing, only, could give her full fellowship with the race. She saw that one thing, only, could make her a link between the ages that were gone and the ages that were to come. That one thing, only, could satisfy her woman heart--could make her feel that she was not alone.

That one thing which the woman recognized as supreme is the thing which the Master of Life has committed peculiarly to womanhood. Not to woman's skillful hands; not to her ready brain; not to the things of her womanhood upon which the world into which she goes alone to labor puts a price has the Master of Life committed this supreme thing; but to her *womanhood*--her sex. In the womanhood that is denied by the world that receives womankind alone, is wealth that may not be bought by any price that the world can pay. In the womanhood of women is that supreme thing without which human life would perish from the earth. The exercise of this power alone can give to woman the high place in Life that belongs to her by right divine. The woman saw that, for her, all other work in the world would be but a makeshift--a substitute; and, because of this, while Life had, never before seemed so large, she had, never before felt so small--so useless.

But still, for the woman, there was peace in her loneliness--there was a peace that she had not had before--there was a calmness, a quietness, that was not hers before her trial. It was the peace of the lonely mountain top to which one climbs from out a noisy, clamoring, village; the calmness of the deep sky uncrossed by cloud or marked by smoke of human industry; the quietness of the wide prairie, untouched by man's improvements. And this tranquil rest was hers because she knew--deep in her woman's heart she knew--that she had done well; that she had not been untrue to the soul of her womanhood.

The woman knew that she had done well because she had come to understand that, while life is placed peculiarly in the care and keeping of her sex, her sex has been endowed, for the protection, perfection, and perpetuation of Life, with peculiar instincts. She had come to understand that, while woman has been made the giver and guardian of Life, she, for that reason, is subject to laws that are not to be broken save with immeasurable loss to the race. To her sex is given, by Life itself, the divine right of selection that the future of the race may be assured. To her sex is given an instinct superior to reason that her choice may perfect human kind. For her, and for the Life of her kind, there is the law that if she permits aught but her woman instinct to influence her in selecting her mate her children and the children of her children shall mourn.

In the crisis of her life the woman had heard many voices--bold and tempting, pleading and subtle--urging her to say: "Yes." But always her instinct--her woman heart--had whispered: "No. This man is not your mate. This is not the man you would choose to be the father of your children. Better, far better, contribute nothing to the race than break the law of your womanhood. Better, far better, never cross the threshold of that open door than cross it with one who, in your heart of hearts you know, to be not the right one."

So the woman had peace. Even in her loneliness, she had peace--knowing that she had done well.

And the woman tried, now, to interest herself in the things that so many of the women of her day seemed to find so interesting. She listened to brave lectures by stalwart women on woman's place and sphere in the world's work. She heard bold talks by militant women about woman's emancipation and freedom. She attended lectures by intellectual women on the higher life, and the new thought, and the advanced ideas. She read pamphlets and books written by modern women on the work of women in the social, political and industrial fields. She became acquainted with many "new" women who, striving mightily with all their strength of body and soul for careers, looked with a kind of lofty disdain or pitying contempt upon those old-fashioned mothers whose children interfere with the duty that "new" women think they owe the world.

But this woman who knew herself to be a woman could not interest herself in these things to which she tried to give attention. She felt that in giving herself to these things she would betray Life. She felt the hollowness, the shallowness, the emptyness of it all in comparison with that which is divinely committed to womankind. She could not but wonder: what would be the racial outcome? When women have long enough substituted other ideals for the ideals of motherhood--other passions for the passions of their sex--other ambitions for the ambition to produce and to perfect Life--other desires for the desire to keep that which Life has committed to them--what then? "How," she asked herself, "would the world get along without mothers? Or how could the race advance if the best of women refused to bear children?" And then came the inevitable thought: are the *best* women, after all, refusing to bear children? Might it not be that the wisdom of Mother Nature is in this also, and that the refusal of a woman to bear children is the best evidence in the world that she is unfit to be a mother? Is it not better that the mothers of the race should be those who hold no ideal, ambition, desire, aim, or purpose in life higher than motherhood? Such women--such mothers--have, thus far, through their sons and daughters, won every victory in Life. It is they who have made every advance of the race possible. Will it not continue to be so, even unto the end? Is not this indeed the law of Life? If there be any work for women greater or of more value to the human race than the work of motherhood then, indeed, is the end of the world, for mankind, at hand.

From where she lay, the woman, when she first awoke that Christmas morning, could see the sun just touching the topmost branches of the tall trees that grew across the street.

It was a beautiful day. But the woman did not at first remember that it was Christmas. Idly, as one sometimes will when awakening out of a deep sleep, she looked at the sunshine on the trees and thought that the day promised to be clear and bright. Then, looking at the clock in the chubby arms of the fat cupid on the mantle, she noticed the time with a start of dismay. She must arise at once or she would be late to her work. Why, she wondered, had not someone called her. Then, a crumpled sheet of tissue paper and a bit of narrow ribbon on the floor, near the table, caught her eye and she remembered.

It was Christmas.

The woman dropped back upon her pillow. She need not go to work that day. She had not been called because it was a holiday. Dully she told herself again that it was Christmas.

The house was very quiet. There were no bare feet pattering down the hall to see what Santa Claus had left from his pack. No exulting shouts had awakened her. In the rooms below, there was no cheerful litter of toys and games and pop corn and candy and nuts with bits of string and crumpled paper from hastily opened parcels and shining scraps of tinsel from the tree. There were no stockings hanging on the mantle. At breakfast, there would be a few friendly gifts and, later, the postman would bring letters and cards with the season's greetings. That was all.

The sun, climbing higher above the tall buildings down town, peeped through the window and saw the woman lying very still. And the sun must have thought that the woman was asleep for her eyes were closed and upon her face there was the wistful smile of a child.

But the woman was not asleep though she was dreaming. She had escaped from the silent, childless, house and had fled far, far, away to a land of golden memories. She had gone back into her Yesterdays--to a Christmas in her Yesterdays.

Once again a little girl, she lived those happy, busy, days of preparation when she had asked herself a thousand times each day: what would the boy give her for Christmas? And always, as she wondered, the little girl had tried not to wish that it would be a doll lest she should be disappointed. And always she was unable to wish, half so earnestly, for anything else. Again she spent the hours learning the song that she was to sing at the church on Christmas eve and wondered, often, if *he* would like her new dress that mother was making for the occasion. And then, as the day drew near, there was that merry trip to the woods to bring the tree, followed by that afternoon at the church. The little girl wondered, that night of the entertainment, if the boy guessed how frightened she was for him lest he forget the words of his part; or, when she was singing before the crowd of people that filled the church, did he know that she saw only him? And then the triumph--the beautiful triumph--of that Christmas morning!

The little girl in the Yesterdays needed no one to remind her what day it was. As soon as it was light, she opened her eyes, and, wide awake in an instant, slipped from her bed to steal down stairs while the rest of the household still slept. And there, in the gray of the winter morning, she found his gift. It was so beautiful, so lifelike, with its rosy cheeks and brown hair that, almost, the little girl was afraid that she was not awake after all; and she caught her breath with a gasp of delight when she finally convinced herself that it was real. She knew that it was from the boy--she *knew*. Quickly she clasped it in her arms, with a kiss and a mother hug; and then, back again she ran to her warm bed lest dolly catch cold. The other presents could wait until it was really, truly, daylight and uncle had made a fire; and she drew the covers carefully up under the dimpled chin of her treasure that lay in the hollow of her arm, close to her own soft little breast, as natural as life--as natural, indeed, as the mother life that throbbed in the heart of the little girl.

For women also it is written: "Except ye become as little children." If only women would understand!

All the other gifts of that Christmas time were as nothing to the little girl beside that gift from the boy. The other things she would enjoy all the more because the supreme wish of her heart had been granted; but, had she been disappointed in *that*, all *else* would have had little power to please. Under all her Christmas pleasure there would have been a longing for something more. Her Christmas would not have satisfied. Her cup of happiness would not have been full. So, all the treasures that the world can lay at woman's feet will never satisfy if the one gift be lacking.

And that woman who has felt in her arms a tiny form moulded of her own flesh--who has drawn close to her breast a soft little cheek and felt upon her neck the touch of a baby hand--that woman knows that I put down the truth when I write that those women who deny the mother instinct of their hearts and, for social position, pleasure, public notice, wealth, or fame, kill their love for children, are to be pitied above all creatures for they deny themselves the heaven that is their inheritance.

Eagerly, that morning, the little girl watched for the coming of the boy for she knew that he would not long delay; and, when she saw him wading through the snow, flung open wide the door to shout her greeting as she proudly held his gift close to her heart; while on her face and in her eyes was the light divine. And great fun they had, that Christmas day, with their toys and games and books; but never for long was the new doll far from the little girl's arms. Nor did she need many words to make her happiness in his gift understood to the boy.

The sun was shining full in the window now; quite determined that the woman should sleep no longer. Regretfully, as one who has little heart for the day, she arose just as footsteps sounded outside her door. Then came a sharp rap upon the panel and--"Merry Christmas"--called her uncle's hearty voice.

Bravely the woman who knew herself to be a woman answered: "Merry Christmas."

DEATH

AND that winter's coat, also, began to appear thin and threadbare.

By looking carefully, one could see that the twigs of the cherry tree were brightening with a delicate touch of fresh color, while the tiny tips of the tender green buds were cautiously peeping out of their snug wrappings as if to ask the state of the weather. In the orchard and the woods, too, the Life that slept deep in the roots and under the bark of trunks and limbs was beginning to stir as though, in its slumber, it heard Spring knocking at its bedroom door.

I do not know what business it was that called the man to a neighboring city. The particular circumstances that made the journey necessary are of no importance whatever to my story. The important thing is this: for the first time the man was forced to recognize, in his own life and in his work, the fact of Death. He came to see that, in the most abundant life, Death cannot be ignored. Because Death is one of the Thirteen Truly Great Things of Life, this is my story: that the man was introduced to Death.

Hurriedly he arranged for his absence, and, rushing home, packed a few necessities of travel in his grip, snatched a hasty dinner, and thus reached the depot just in time to catch the evening train. He would make the trip in the night, devote the following day to the business that demanded his presence, and the next night would return to his home city.

The Pullmans were well filled, mostly with busy, eager, men who, like himself, were traveling at night to save the daylight for their work. But the man, perhaps because he was tired with the labor of the day or because he wished to have for the business of the morrow a clear, vigorous, brain, made no effort to find acquaintances who might be on the train or to meet congenial strangers with whom to spend a pleasant hour. When he had read the evening papers and had outlined in his mind a plan of operation to meet the situation that compelled him to make the hurried trip, he retired to his berth.

The low, monotonous, hum of the flying wheels on the heavy steel rails; the steady, easy, motion of the express as it flew over the miles of well ballasted track; the dim light of the curtained berth, and the quiet of the Pullman, soon lulled the tired traveler to sleep. Mile after mile and mile after mile was marked off, with the steady regularity of time itself, by the splendidly equipped train as it rushed through the darkness with its sleeping passengers. Hamlets, villages, way stations, signal towers, were passed with flash like quickness; while the veteran in the engine cab, with the schooling of thirty years in the hand that rested on the throttle, gazed steadily ahead to catch, with quick eye and clear brain, the messages of the signal lamps that, like bright colored dots of a secret code, appeared on the black sheet of night.

With a suddenness that defies description, the change came.

The trained eyes that looked from the cab window read a message from Death in the night ahead. In the fractional part of a second, the hand on the throttle responded, doing in flash like movements all that the thirty years had taught it to do. There was a frightful jarring, jolting crash of grinding, screaming, brakes, followed on the instant by a roaring, smashing, thundering, rending of iron and steel and wood.

The veteran, whose eye and brain and hand had been thirty years in service, lay under his engine, a mangled, inanimate mass of flesh; His fireman, who had looked forward to a place on the engineer's side of a cab as a young soldier dreams of sword and shoulder straps, lay still beside his chief. From the wrecked coaches, above the sound of hissing steam and crackling flames, came groans and shrieks and screams of tortured men and women and children.

Then, quickly, the hatless, coatless, and half dressed forms of the more fortunate ones ran here and there. Voices were heard calling and answering. There were oaths and prayers and curses mingled with sharp spoken commands and the sound of axes and saws and sledges, as the men, who a few minutes before were sleeping soundly in their berths, toiled with superhuman energy to free their fellows from that horrid hell.

To the man who had escaped from the trap of death that had caught so many of his fellow passengers and who toiled now with the strength of a giant among the rescuers, it all seemed a dream of terror from which he must presently awake. He did not think, then, of the Death that had come so close while he slept. He was not conscious of the danger that had threatened him. He did not feel gratitude for his escape. He could not think. He could only strive madly, with the strength of despair, in the fight to snatch others from the grip of an awful fate; and, as he fought, he prayed to be awakened from his dream.

It was over at last.

Hours later, the man reached his destination, and still, because his business was so urgent, there was no time for him to think of the Death that had come so close. Rarely does the business of life give men time to think of the Death that stands never far away. But, when his work was finished and he was again aboard the train, on his way home, there was opportunity for a fuller realization of the danger through which he had passed so narrowly-- there was time to think. Then it was that the man realized a new thing in his life. Then it was that a new factor entered into his thinking--Death. Not the knowledge of Death; he had always had that of course. Not the fear of Death; this man was no coward. But the *fact* of Death--it was the *fact* of Death that he realized now as he had never realized it before.

All unexpected and unannounced--without sign of its approach or warning of its presence--Death had stood over him. He had looked into the eyes of the King. Death had touched him on the shoulder, as it were, and had passed on. But Death would come again. The one firmly fixed, undeniable, unalterable, fact in Life was, to him, now, that Death would come again. When or how; that, he could not know; perhaps not for many years; perhaps before the flying train could carry him another mile. How strange it is that this one fixed, permanent, unalterable, inevitable fact of Life--Death--is most commonly ignored. The most common thing in Life is Death; yet few there are who recognize it as a fact until it presents itself saying: "Come."

Going back into the years, the man recalled the death of his mother; and, later, when he was standing on the very threshold of his manhood, the death of his father. Those graves on the hillside were still in his memory but they had not realized Death for him. His grief at the loss of those so dear to him had overshadowed, as it were, the fact of Death itself. He thought of Death only as it had taken his parents; he did not consider it in thinking of himself. But now--now--he had looked into the eyes of the King. He had felt the touch of the hand that chills. He had heard the voice that cannot be disobeyed. Death had come into his life a *fact*.

The low, steady, hum and whirr of the wheels and the smooth, easy movement of the train told him of the flying miles. One by one, those miles that lay between him and the end of his journey would go until the last was gone and he would step from the coach to the platform of his home depot. And, then, all suddenly, to the man, those flying miles became as the years of his life. Even as the miles of his journey were passing so his years had gone--so his years were going and would go.

The man was a young man still. For the first time, he felt himself growing old. Involuntarily he looked at his hands; firm, strong, young hands they were, but the man, in his fancy, saw them shaking, withered, and parched, with prominent dull blue veins, and the skinny fingers bent and crooked with the years. He glanced down at his powerful, full moulded limbs, and, in fancy, saw them thin and shrunken with age. And, suddenly, he remembered with a start that the next day would be his birthday. In the fullness of his young manhood's strength, he had ignored the passing years even as he had ignored Death. As he had learned to forget Death, he had learned to forget his birthdays. It was strange how fast the years were going, thought the man. Scarcely would there be time for the working out of his dreams.

And, once, it had been such a long, long, time between his birthdays. Once, he had counted the months, then the weeks, then the days that lay between. Once, he remembered--

Perhaps it was the thought of his birthday that did it; perhaps it was the memory of those graves in the old cemetery at home. Whatever it was, the man slipped back into his Yesterdays when birthdays were ages and ages apart and, more than anything else in the world, the boy wanted to grow up.

At seven, he had looked with envy upon the boy of nine while the years of grown up men were beyond his comprehension. At nine, fifteen was the daring limit of his dreams; so far away it seemed that scarcely he hoped to reach it. As for eighteen--one must be very, very, old, indeed, to be eighteen. How long the years ahead had seemed, *then*--and *now*, how short they were when looking back! And the birthdays--the birthdays that the man had learned to forget--how could he have learned to forget them! What days of triumph--what times of victorious rejoicing--those days once had been! And so, with the fact of Death so recently forced into his life, with the miles as years slipping under the fast whirring wheels that bore him onward, the man lived again a birthday in the long ago.

Weeks before that day the boy had planned the joyous occasion, for mother had promised that he should have a party. A birthday party! Joyous festival of the Yesterdays! What delightful hours were spent in anticipation! What innumerable questions were asked! What a multitude of petitions were formed and presented! What anxious consultations with the little girl who lived next door! What suggestions were offered, accepted and rejected, and rejected or accepted all over again! What lists of the guests to be invited were made, revised and then revised again! What counting of the days, and, as the day drew near, what counting of the hours; not forgetting, all the time, to hint, in various skillfully persuasive and suggestive ways, as to the presents that would be most fitting and acceptable! And at last, when the day had come, as all days must at last come, was there ever in the history of mortal man or boy such a day?

There was real wealth of love in mother's kiss that morning. There was holy pleasure in the pride that was in father's face and voice. There was unmarred joy when the little girl captured him and, while he pretended--only pretended--to escape, gave him the required number of thumps on the back with her soft little fist and the triumphant "one to grow on." Then came, at last, the crowning event: and so the man saw, again, the boys and girls who, that afternoon in his Yesterdays, helped to celebrate his birthday. Why had he permitted them to pass out of his life? Why had he gone out of their lives? Why must the years rob him of the friends of the Yesterdays?

With the birthday feast of good things and the games and sports of childhood the busy afternoon passed. Up and down the road and across the fields, the guests departed, with their party dresses soiled, their party combed hair disheveled, and their party cleaned faces smudged with grime; but with the clean, clean, joy of the Yesterdays in their clean, clean, childish hearts. Together the boy and the girl watched them go, with waving hands and good-bye shouts, until the last one had passed from sight and the last whoop and call had died away. And then, reluctantly, the little girl herself went home and the boy was left alone by the garden hedge.

Oh, brave, brave, day of the Yesterdays! Brave birthdays of the long ago when Death was not a fact but a fiction! When the years were ages apart, and the farthest reach of one's imagination carried only to being grown up!

From his Yesterdays the man came back to wonder: if Death should wait until he was wrinkled, bent, and old--until his limbs were palsied, his hearing gone, his voice cracked and shrill, and his eyes dim--if Death should let him stay until he had seen the last of his companions go home in the evening after that last birthday--would there be one to stand beside him--to watch with him as the others passed from sight? Would there be anyone to help him celebrate his last birthday, if Death should fail to come again until he was old?

* * * * *

Everyone was very kind to the woman that morning when the word came that her uncle had been killed in a railroad accident. All that kind hearts could do for her was done. Every offer of assistance was made. But there was really nothing that anyone could do just then. She must first go as quickly as she could to her aunt.

The man of authority, who had always seemed to understand her woman heart and who had paid to her the highest tribute possible for a man to pay a woman, had broken the news to her as gently as news of Death can be told, and, as soon as she was ready, his own carriage was waiting before the entrance in the street below. Nor did he burden her with talk as they were driven skillfully through the stream of the down town traffic and then, at a quicker pace, through the more open streets of the residence district.

There is so little that can be said, even by the most thoughtful, when Death enters thus suddenly into a life. The man knew that the woman needed him. He knew that, save for the invalid aunt, there was now no near relative to help her do the necessary things that must be done. There was no one to help her think what would be best to do. So he asked her gently, as they neared the house, if she would not permit him, for the next few days, to take the place in her life that would have been taken by an older brother. Kindly he asked that she trust him fully--that she let him think and do for her--be a help to her in her need--even as he would have helped her had she consented to come into his life as he wished her to come. And the woman, because she knew the goodness and honor of this man's heart, thanked him with gratitude too great for words and permitted him to do for her all that a most intimate relative would have done.

At last it was over. The first uncontrollable expressions of grief--the arrangements for the funeral--the service at the house and the long ride to the cemetery with the final parting and the return to the house that would never again be quite the same--all those hard, first, days were past and to-morrow--to-morrow--the woman would go back to her work. In the final going over of affairs, the finishing of unfinished business, the ending of undeveloped plans and prospects, the settling and closing of accounts, and the considering of new conditions enforced by Death, it had been made very clear that for the woman to work was, now, more than ever necessary. There was, now, no one but her upon whom the invalid aunt could depend for even the necessities of life.

And the woman was glad that she was able to provide for that one who had always been so gentle, so patient, in suffering and who, in her sorrow, was now so brave. Since the death of the girl's own mother, the aunt had taken, so far as she could, a mother's place in the life of the child; and, as the years had passed and the little girl had grown into young womanhood, she had grown into the heart of the childless woman until she was as a daughter of her own flesh. So the woman did not feel this added care that was forced upon her by the changed conditions as a burden other than a burden of love. But still, that afternoon, when it was all over, and she faced the new future that Death had set before her, she realized the fact of Death as she had never realized it before.

The years since her mother's death had not been many, and, it seemed to her, now, that they had passed very quickly. She was only a little girl, then, and her uncle and his wife had taken her so fully into their hearts that she had scarcely felt the gap in her life after the first weeks of the separation had passed. Her mother belonged to the days of her childhood and, though the years were not many as she looked back, those childhood days seemed far, far, away. Death had come to her, now, in the days of her womanhood. Suddenly, unexpectedly, with awful, startling, reality, the fact of Death had come into her life; forcing her to consider, as she had never considered before, the swiftly passing years.

What--she asked herself as she thought of the morrow--what, for her, lay at the farthermost end of that procession of to-morrows? When the best of her strength was gone with the days and weeks and months and years--what then? When Death should come for that one who was, in everything but blood, her mother and who was, now, her only companion--what then? To be left alone in the world--to go, alone, all the rest of the journey--this was the horror that Death brought to her. As she looked, that afternoon, into the years that were to come, this woman, who knew that she was a woman, and who was still in the glory and beauty of her young womanhood, felt suddenly old--she felt as though every day of the sad days just passed had been a year.

And then, at last, from her grief of the present and from her contemplation of the years that were to come, she turned wearily back to the long ago. In the loneliness and sorrow of her life she went, again, back into her Yesterdays. There was, indeed, no other place for her to go but back into her Yesterdays. Only in the Yesterdays can one escape the sadness and loneliness that attend the coming of Death. Death has little power in the Yesterdays. In childhood life, Death is not a fact.

Funerals were nothing more than events of surpassing interest in those days--a subdued, intense, interest that must not be too openly expressed, it is true, but that nevertheless could not be altogether suppressed. Absorbed in her play the little girl would hear, suddenly, the ringing of the bell in the white church across the valley; and it would ring, not joyously, cheerily, interestingly, as on Sundays but with sad, solemn, measured, notes, that would fill her childish heart with hushed excitement. And then--it mattered not where he was or what he was doing--the little boy would come, rushing with eager haste, to join her at the front gate where they always watched together for the procession and strove for the honor of sighting first the long string of vehicles that would soon appear on one of the four roads leading to the church. And oh, joy of joys, if it so happened that the procession came by the way that led past the place where they danced with such eager impatience!

First would come, moving with slow feet and drooping head, the old gray horse and time worn phaeton of the minister; and they would feel a little strange and somewhat hurt because the man of God, who usually greeted them so cheerily, would not notice them as he passed. But the sadness in their hearts would be forgotten the next moment as they gazed, with excited interest and whispered exclamations, at the shining, black, hearse with its beautiful, coal black, horses that, stepping proudly, tossing their plumed heads, and shaking the tassels on the long nets that hung over their glossy sides, seemed to invite the admiration that greeted them. And then, through the glass sides of the hearse, the boy and the girl, with gasps of interest, would discover the long black coffin half hidden by its load of flowers; or, perhaps, the hearse, the horses, and the coffin, would all be snow white which, the little girl thought, was prettiest of all. Then would follow the long line of carriages, filled with people who wore their Sunday clothes; and the boy and the girl, recognizing a friend or acquaintance, here and there, would wonder to themselves how it would seem to be riding in such a procession. One by one, they would count the vehicles and recall the number in the last funeral they had watched; gleefully triumphant, if this procession were longer than the last; scornfully disappointed, if it were not so imposing. And then, when the last carriage had gone up the hill on the other side of the creek and had disappeared from sight among the trees that half hid the church, they would wait for the procession to reappear after the services and would watch it crawling slowly along the distant road on its way to the cemetery.

And the next day they would play a funeral.

Even as they had played a wedding, they would play a funeral. Only, they played a wedding but that once, while they played funerals many, many, times.

Sometimes it would be a doll's funeral when the chief figure in the solemn rites would be taken from the grave, after it was all over, and would be rocked to sleep with the other dollies, none the worse, apparently, for the sad experience. Again, the part of the departed would be taken by a mouse that had met a violent death at the hands of the cook; or, perhaps, they would find a baby bird that had fallen from its nest before its wings were strong. But the grandest, most triumphant, most successful funeral of the Yesterdays was a kitten that had most opportunely died the very day a real grown up funeral had passed the house. What a funeral that was--with an old shoe box for a coffin, the boy's wagon draped with pieces of black cloth borrowed from the rag bag for a hearse, the shepherd dog for a proudly stepping team, and all the dolls in their carriage following slowly behind! In a corner of the garden, not far from the cherry tree, they dug a real grave and set up a real tombstone, fashioned by the boy, to mark the spot. And the little girl was so earnest in her sorrow that she cried real tears at which the boy became, suddenly, very gay and boisterous, as boys will upon such occasions, and helped her to forget right quickly.

Oh, boy of the Yesterdays, who would not let his little girl mate grieve but made her laugh and forget! Where was he now? The woman wondered. Had Death come into his life, too? Were the years ever, to him, as a funeral procession? Did ever he feel that he was growing old? Could he, now, make her forget her grief--could he help her to laugh again--or had his power gone even as those Yesterdays when Death, too, was only a pleasing game?

From the next room, a gentle voice called softly and the woman arose to go to her aunt. For that one who was left dependent upon her she would be brave and strong--she would go back to her work in the morning.

Only children are privileged to play with the fact of Death. Only in the Yesterdays are funerals events of merely passing interest. Only in the Yesterdays does Death go always past the door.

FAILURE

AND that year, also, went to join the years of the Yesterdays.

It is as though Life, bringing to man every twelve months a new year, bids him try again. Always, it is necessary for man to try again. Indeed Life itself is nothing less than this: a continual trying again.

In the world laboratory, mankind is conducting a series of elaborate experiments--always on the verge of the great discovery but never quite making it--always thinking that the secret is about to be revealed but never quite uncovering it--always failing in his experiments but always finding in the process something that leads him, with hope renewed, to try again.

The man had failed.

Sadly, sternly, with the passing of the year, he admitted to himself that he had failed. Humiliated and ashamed, with the coming of the new year, he admitted that he must begin again. Bitterly he called himself a fool. And perhaps he was--more or less. Most men are a little foolish. The man who has never been forced to swallow his own folly has missed a bitter but wholesome tonic that, more than likely, he needs. This man was not the kind of a man who would blame any one but himself for his failure. If he had been that particular kind of a fool his failure would have been of little value either to him or to any one. Neither would there be, for me, a story.

I do not know the particulars of this man's failure--neither the what, the why, nor the how. I know only that he failed--that it was necessary for him to fail. Nor is this a story of such particulars for they are of little importance. A man can fail in anything. Some, even, seem to fail in everything. This, therefore, is my story: that as Failure enters into the life of every man it came into the life of this man. In some guise or other Failure seems to be a necessity. It is one of the Thirteen Truly Great Things of Life. But the man did not, at that time, understand that his failure was a necessity. *That* understanding came to him only with Success.

You may say that this man was too young to accomplish a real Failure. But you need not bother about that, either. One is never too young to experience Failure. And Failure, to the one who fails, is always, at the time, very real.

So this man saw the castles that he had toiled so hard to build come tumbling down about him. So he was awakened from his bright dreams to find that they were only dreams. So he came to see his work as idleness and folly. Sorrowfully he looked at the ruin of his building. Hopelessly he recalled his dreams. Despairingly he looked upon his fruitless labor. With his fine manhood's strength dead within him, he bitterly felt himself to be but a weakling; fit only to be pushed aside by the stronger, better, men among whom he went, now, with lifeless step and downcast face. There was left in his heart no courage and no hope. He saw himself a most miserable coward, and, ashamed and disgraced in his own sight, he shrank from the eyes of his fellows and withdrew into himself to hide.

And the only thing that saved the man was this: he did not pity himself. Self-pity is debilitating. It is the dry rot that weakens the life lines. It is the rust that eats the anchor chains. At the last analysis, a man probably knows less about himself than he knows about others. The only difference is that what he knows about others is sometimes right while that which he thinks he knows about himself is nearly always wrong. Salvation is in pitying someone else. If one must have pity he should accept it from strangers only. The pity of strangers is harmless to the object of it and very gratifying--to the strangers. Self-accusation, self-censure, self-condemnation: these are the antidotes for the poison that sometimes enters the soul through Failure. But these antidotes must be administered with care. Self-accusation has, usually, a very low percentage of cause. Self-censure, undiluted, is dangerous to self-respect. And self-condemnation is rarely to be had pure. When one brings himself to trial before himself his chance for justice is small--the judge is nearly always prejudiced, the jury packed, and the evidence incomplete.

The man, when he had withdrawn into himself, saw the world moving on its way without him as though his failure mattered, to it, not at all. He was forced to realize that the work of the world could be done without him. He was compelled to see that the sum of human happiness and human woe would be neither less nor more because of him. The world did not really need his success--he needed it. The world did not suffer from his failure--he suffered. He did not understand, then, that no man is in line for success until he understands how little either his success or his failure matters to the world. He did not know, then, how often a good strong failure is the corner stone of a well builded life.

A child is not crippled for life because it falls when it is learning to walk; neither has a man come to the end of his upward climb because he "stubs his toe." The man knew this later but just then he was too sore at heart to think of even trying to get up again. All those first months of that new year he did nothing but the labor that was necessary for him to do in order to live. And, in that which he did, he had no heart but toiled as a dumb beast toils in obedience to its master. The joy of work which is the reward of labor was gone.

So the spring came. The air grew warm and balmy. The grass on the lawns and in the parks began to look soft and inviting to feet that were weary with the feel of icy pavements. The naked trees were being clothed in spring raiment, fresh and green. The very faces of the people seemed to glow with a new warmth as though a more generous life was stirring in their veins. As the sun gathered strength, and the coldness and bleakness of winter retreated farther and farther before the advance of summer, the manner and dress of the crowds upon the streets marked the change as truly as the habits of the birds and flowers, until, at last, here and there, straw hats appeared and suddenly, as bluebirds come, barefooted boys were playing marbles in the alleys and fishing tackle appeared in the windows of the stores.

All his life the man had been an ardent fisherman. And so, when his eyes were attracted that noon, as he was passing one of those windows filled with rods and reels and lines and hooks and nets and all things dear to the angler's heart, he paused. His somber face brightened. His form, that was already stooped a little, straightened. His listless eyes, for a moment, shone with their old time fire. Then he went on to his work.

But, less than ever, that afternoon, was the man's heart in his labor. While his hands mechanically performed their appointed tasks and his brain as mechanically did its part, the man himself was not there. He had gone far, far, away into his Yesterdays. Once again, in his Yesterdays, the man went fishing.

The boy was a very small boy when first he went fishing. And he fished in the brook that ran through the valley below the little girl's house. His hook was only a pin, bent by his own fingers; his line, a bit of string or thread borrowed from mother's work basket; and his rod, a slender branch of willow or a green shoot from one of the trees in the orchard, or, it might be, a stalk of the tall pigweed that grew down behind the barn; and for bait, those humble friends of boyhood, the angle worms. How the boy shouted and danced with glee when he found a big one; even though he did shudder a little as he picked it up, squirming and wiggling, to drop it into the old baking powder can he called his bait box! And how the little girl shrieked with fear and admiration! Very proud was the boy that he had courage to handle the crawling things--though many of them did escape into their tiny holes before he could bring himself quite to the point of catching them and pulling them out. "Only girls are afraid of worms and toads and bugs. Boys can bait their own hooks." Manfully, too, did he hide his thoughts when conscience pricked him, even as he the worm. "Do worms have feelin's?" He wondered. "Does it hurt?" Half frightened, he had laughed, one day, when the little girl asked: "What if some wicked giant should catch you and stick you on a great hook and swing you through the air, kicking and squirming, and drop you into the water where it's deep, and leave you there till some great fish comes along to swallow you like the man in the Bible that mother reads about?"

But the boy in his Yesterdays carried home no fish from that little brook; though he spent many hours in the hot summer sun watching eagerly for a bite. He knew there must be fish there--great big fellows--there were such lovely places for them under the grassy banks--if only they would come out--but they never did. Not until he was older did the boy understand the real reason of this failure. The water was not deep enough. He learned, in time, that big fish are not found in shallow streams.

I do not know, but perhaps, the man, even as the boy, was fishing in a too shallow stream.

As he grew older, the boy wandered farther down the creek. A "sure 'nough" fishhook took the place of the bent pin and a real "boughten" line, with a sinker, was tied to the hook though he still used the slender willow rods. And, now, he sometimes brought home a fish or two from the deeper water down in the pasture lot; and no success in after life would ever bring to the man the same thrill of delight that was felt by the boy when he landed a tiny "chub" or "shiner." No Roman general, returning in triumph from the wars with captives chained to his chariot, ever moved with a prouder spirit than he, when he went home to mother with his little string of captured fishes.

Then there came a day that was the proudest in his life--the day when he was given a larger hook, a longer line, a cane pole, and permission to go to the mill pond. No more fishing for him in the brook now! He had outgrown all that. How small the little stream seemed, now, as he crossed it on his way down the road! Could it be possible, he asked himself, that he was ever content to fish there, and with a bent pin, at that? And he felt carefully in his pocket to see if those extra hooks were safe; and took another peep at the big worms in his bait box--an old tomato can this time. There would be no twinge of conscience when he baited his hook that day. And proudly he tried to take longer steps in the dusty road; almost breaking into a run as he neared the turn where he knew that he would see the pond.

Often, the boy wondered if there could be anywhere in all the world such another body of water as that old mill pond. Often, he wondered how deep it was down by the dam in the shadow of the giant elms that half hid the mill. Many times, he questioned: "Where did all the water come from anyway?" Surely it could not *all* come from the tiny stream that flowed down the valley below the little girl's house! Why, he could wade in that and there were boats on this!

Once again, the man, in his Yesterdays, stood at that turn in the road; under his bare, boyish, feet the hot, hot, dust; over his head the blue, blue, sky; before him the beautiful water that mirrored back the trees, the clouds, and the buildings. Once again, he sat in the shadow of the old covered bridge, fish pole in hand, and, with boyish delight and pride, hailed each addition to the string of catfish and suckers that swam near by, safely anchored to the bank. He could hear the drowsy hum of the mill across the pond and the merry shout of the miller hailing some passer-by. And, now and then, would come, the clatter of horses' hoofs and the rumble of a farmer's wagon on the planks above his head and he would idly watch the ever widening circles in the water as some bit of dirt, jarred from the beams above, marred the glassy surface. The swallows were wheeling here and there in swift, graceful motions; one moment lightly skimming the surface of the pond and the next, high in air above the trees and buildings. A water snake came gliding toward an old log close by. A turtle was floating lazily in the sun. And a kingfisher startled him with its harsh, discordant, rattle as it passed in rapid flight toward the upper end of the pond where the tall cat-tails were nodding in the sunlight and the drooping willows fringed the bank with green.

The shadows of the giant elms near the dam grew longer and longer. A workman left the mill and started across the pasture toward his home. A farmer stopped on his way from the field to water his team. The frogs began to call shrilly from the reeds and rushes. The swallows, twittering, sought their nests beneath the bridge. It was time that the boy was going home.

Slowly, reluctantly, the little fisherman drew his line from the water and wrapped it carefully round the pole. Then, picking up his string of fish, he inspected them thoughtfully--admiring the largest and wishing that the others were like him--and, casting one last glance at the water, the trees, the mill, started down the road toward home.

He must hurry now. It was later than he thought. Mother would be watching and waiting supper for him. How pleased she would be to see his fish. He wished that the string were longer. How quickly the night was coming on. It was almost dark. And then, as the boy went down into the deepening dusk of the valley, he saw, on the other side, the light in the windows. He was almost home.

Tired little fisherman. Wearily he crossed the creek and made his way up the gentle slope toward the lights that gleamed so brightly against the dark mass of the orchard hill, while high above, the first stars of the evening were coming out. And then, as in the gloaming he reached at last the gate where the little girl lived, he found her waiting--watching anxiously--eager to greet him with sweet solicitude. "Did you catch anything?"

Proudly the boy exhibited his catch--wishing again in his heart that the string were longer. Sadly, he told how the biggest fish of all had dropped from his hook just when he had it almost landed. And sometimes--the man remembered--sometimes the boy was forced to answer that he had caught nothing at all. But always, then, would he bravely declare that he would have better luck next time.

Tired little fisherman--going home with his catch in the evening! Always--disappointed little fisherman--wishing that his string were longer! Always-brave-to-try-again little fisherman--when his day was a day of failure!

The man came back from his Yesterdays, that afternoon, to wonder: when the shadows of his life grew longer and longer--when his sun was slowly setting--when he reluctantly withdrew, at last, from the busy haunts of men--when he went down the road toward home, as it grew darker and darker until he could not see the way, would there be a light in the window for him? Would he know that someone was waiting and watching? And would he wish that his string of fish were longer? However great his catch, would he not wish that the string were longer? And might it not be, too, that always in life the largest fish would be the one that he had almost landed?

And it was so that the old fire came again into the man's eyes to stay. He stood once more erect before men. Again his countenance was lighted with courage and with hope. With the brave words of the little fisherman who had caught nothing, the man, once again, faced the world to work out his dreams.

* * * * *

And the woman who knew herself to be a woman was haunted by the thought of Failure.

After Death had come with such suddenness into her life, she had gone back to her work, and, in spite of the changes that Death had wrought, the days had gone much as the days before. But, because of the new conditions and the added responsibilities, she gave herself, now, somewhat more fully to that work than she had ever done before. She left for herself less time for the dreams of her womanhood--less time for waiting beside that old, old, door beyond which lay the life that she desired with all the strength of her woman heart.

And that world in which she labored--that life to which she now gave herself more and more--rewarded her more and more abundantly. Because she was strong in body with skillful hands and quick brain; because she was superior in these things to many who labored beside her; she received a larger reward than they. For the richness, the fullness, of her womanhood, she received nothing. From love, the only thing that can make that which a woman receives fully acceptable to her, she received nothing.

There were many who, now, congratulated the woman upon what they called her success. And some, who knew the measure of the reward she received from the world that set a price upon the things of her womanhood, envied her; wishing themselves as fortunate as she. She was even pointed out and spoken of triumphantly, by certain modern, down-to-date, ones, as an example of the successful woman of the age. Her success--as it was called--was cited as a triumphant argument for the right of women to sell their womanhood for a price: to put their strength of mind and flesh and blood, their physical and intellectual vigor, their vitality and life, upon a market that cannot recognize their womanhood; even though by so doing they rob the race of the only contribution they can make that will add to its perfection.

Really, if the customs and necessities of this age of "down-to-date-ism" are to take the world's mothers, then it would seem that this age of "down-to-date-ism" should find, for the perpetuation and perfection of the race, a substitute for women. The age should evolve a better way, a more modern method, than the old-fashioned way that has been in vogue so long. For, just as surely as the laws of life are beyond our power to repeal, so surely will the operation of the laws of life not change to accommodate our newest thinking and the race, by spending its best woman strength in work that cannot recognize womanhood, will bequeath to the ages to come an ever lowering standard of human life.

The woman felt this--she felt that she could most truly serve the race by being true to the dreams of her womanhood. She felt that the work she was doing was not her real work but a makeshift to be undertaken under protest and discarded without regret when her opportunity to enter upon the real work of her life should present itself. But still, even while feeling this, gradually there had come to be, for her, an amount of satisfaction in knowing that she was succeeding in that which she had set her hand to do. In the increasing reward she received, in the advanced position she occupied, in the deference that was shown her, in the authority that was given her, in the larger interests that were intrusted to her, and even in the attitude of those who held her to be a convincing example of the newest womanhood, there was coming to be a kind of satisfaction.

Then came that day when the woman expressed a little of this satisfaction to the man who had always understood and who had been always so kind. In this, too, the woman felt that he understood.

The man had not sought to take advantage of the intimacy she had granted him in those trying days when Death had come into her life. He had never failed in being kind and considerate in the thousand little things of the work that brought them together and that gave her opportunity to learn his goodness and the genuine worth of his manhood. Nor had he failed to make her understand that still he hoped for the time when she would go with him into the life beyond the old, old, door. But that day, when she made known to him, a little, her growing satisfaction in that which the world called her success, she saw that he was hurt. For the first time he seemed to be troubled and afraid for her.

Very gravely lie looked down into her eyes. Very gravely he congratulated her. And then, quietly and convincingly, with words of authority, he pointed out to her the possible heights she might reach--would reach--if she continued. He told her of the place that she, if she chose, might gain. He spoke of the reward that would be hers. And, as he talked to her of these things, he saw the light of interest and anticipation kindling in her eyes. Sadly he saw it. Then, pausing--hesitating--he asked her slowly: "Do you really think that it is, after all, worth while? For *you*, I mean, do you think that it would be a satisfying success?" He did not wish to interfere with her career, he said--and smiled a little at the word. He would even help her if--if--she was sure that such a career would bring her the real happiness he so much wanted her to have.

And the woman, as the man looked into her eyes and as she saw the trouble in his thoughtful face and listened to his gravely spoken words, felt ashamed. Remembering, again, the dreams of her womanhood, she was ashamed. From that day, the woman was haunted by the thought of Failure.

Why, she asked herself, why could she not open the door of her heart to this man who had been so good to her--so true to her and to himself? If he had taken advantage in any way, if he had sought to use his power, she would not have cared so much. But because she knew him so well; because she had seen his splendid character, his fine manhood, his kindness of heart, and his strength; because of the dreams of her womanhood; she had tried to open the door and bid him take possession of her heart that was as an empty room furnished and ready. But she could not. She seemed to have lost the key. Why--why--could she not give this man what he asked? Why could she not go with him into the life of her dreams? What was it that held her back? What was it that held shut the door of her womanhood against him? Could it be that, after all, she was fit only for the career upon which she was already entered? Could it be that she was not worthy to enter into the life her womanhood craved--the life for which she had longed with such passionate longing--the life she had desired with such holy desire? Could it be that she was unworthy of her womanhood?

Bitterly this woman, who knew herself to be a woman, who

had dreamed the dreams of womanhood, and who was pointed out as a successful woman--bitterly she felt that she had failed.

She knew that her failure could not be because she had squandered the wealth of her womanhood. Very carefully had she kept the treasures of her womanhood for the coming of that one for whom she waited--knowing not who he was but only that she would know him when he came. Might it be that he *had* come and she did not know him? Might it be that the heart of her womanhood did not know? If this was so then, indeed, Life itself is but an accident and must trust to blind chance the fulfillment of its most sacred mission--the perpetuation and perfection of itself.

That the Creator should give laws for the right mating of all his creatures except man--leaving men and women, alone, with no guide to lead them aright in this relationship that is most vital to the species--is unthinkable. Deeply implanted in the hearts of men and women there is, also, an instinct; an instinct that is superior to the dictates of the social, financial, or ecclesiastical will. And it is this natural instinct of mate selection that should govern the marriages of human kind as truly as it marries the birds of the fields and the wild things that mate in the forests.

The woman knew, instinctively, that she should not give herself to this man. She felt in her heart that to do so would make her kin to her sisters in the unnamable profession. The church would sanction, the state would legalize, and society would accept such a union--does accept such unions--but only the divine laws of Life, given for the protection of Life, can ever make a man and a woman husband and wife. The laws that govern the right mating of human kind are not enacted by organizations either social, political, or religious, but are written in the hearts of those who would, in mating, fulfill the purpose of Life. These laws may be broken by man but they cannot by him be repealed; and the penalty that is imposed for their violation is very evident to all who have eyes to see and who observe with understanding.

The woman knew, also, that, in respect and honor and gratitude to this man, she dared not do this thing against which the instinct of her heart protested. But still she asked herself: "Why? Why was the door shut against him? Why was it not in her power to do that which she so longed to do?"

And still, the thought of Failure haunted her.

And so it was, that, in asking, "why"--in seeking the reason of her failure, the woman was led back even to the years of her childhood. Back into her Yesterdays she went in search of the key that kept fast locked the door of her heart against the man whom she would have so gladly admitted. And, all the way back, as she retraced the steps of her years, she looked for one who might have the key. But she found no one. And in her Yesterdays she found only a boy who had entered her heart when it was the heart of a little girl.

That the boy of her Yesterdays lived still in the heart of the woman, she knew. But surely--surely--the boy was not strong enough to hold her woman heart against the man who sought admittance. The boy could not hold the door against the man and against the woman herself. Those vows, made so solemnly under the cherry tree, were but childish vows. It was but a play wedding, after all. And the kiss that had sealed the vows--the kiss that was so different from other kisses--it was but a childish kiss ... In the long years that had come between that boy and girl the vows and the kiss had become but memories--even as the games they played--even as her keeping house and her family of dolls. That child wedding belonged only to the Yesterdays.

The woman was haunted by the thought of Failure.

SUCCESS

THE world said that he was a young man to have achieved so notable a Success. And he was. But years have, really, little to do with a man's age. It is the use that a man makes of his years that ages him or keeps him young.

This man knew that he was a man. He knew that manhood is not a matter of years. And, knowing this, he had dreamed a man's dream. In the world he had found something to do--a man's work--and from his Occupation he had gained Knowledge. He had learned the value of Ignorance and, behind the things that men have hung upon and piled about it, he had come to recognize Religion. He knew both the dangers and the blessings of Tradition. He had gained the heights that are fortified by Temptation and from those levels so far above the lowlands had looked out upon Life. Death he knew as a fact and through Failure he had passed as through a smelting furnace. It is these things, I say, that count for more in life than years. So, although he was still young, the man was ready for Success. He was in the fullness of his manhood strength. The tide of Life, for him, was just reaching its height.

I do not know just what it was in which the man achieved Success. Just what it was, indeed, is not my story; nor does it matter for Success is always the same. My story is this: that the man achieved Success while he was still young and strong to rejoice in the triumph.

The dreams that he had dreamed on the hilltop, when first he realized his manhood, were, in part, fulfilled. He was looked upon by the world as one not of the common herd--as one not of the rank and file. He was accepted, in the field of his work, as a leader--a master. He was held as one having authority and power. The world pointed him out to its children as an example to be followed. The mob, that crowds always at the foot of the ladder, looked up and cursed or begged or praised as is the temper of such mobs. His name was often in the papers. When he appeared on the streets or in public places he was recognized. The people told each other who he was and what he had done. He was received as a companion by those who were counted great by the world. Doors that were closed to the multitude, and that had been closed to him, were opened readily. Opportunities, offered only to the few, were presented. The golden stream of wealth flowed to his feet. By the foolish hangers-on of the world he was sought--he was offered praise and admiration. All that is called Success, in short, was his; not in so great a measure as had come to some older than he, it is true; but it was genuine; it was merited; it was secure; and, with the years, it would increase as a river nearing the sea.

And the man, as he looked back to that day of his dreams, was glad with an honest gladness. As he looked back to the time when he had asked of the world only something to do, he was proud with a just pride. As he looked back upon the things out of which he had builded his Success and saw how well he had builded, he was satisfied. But still in his gladness and pride and satisfaction there was a disappointment.

In his dreams, when he had looked out upon the world as a conquering emperor, the man had seen only the deeds of valor--the exhibitions of courage, of heroism, of strength--he had seen only the victories--the honors. But now, in the fulfillment of his dreams--when he had won the victory--when the honors were his--he knew the desperate struggle, the disastrous losses, the pitiful suffering. He had felt the dangers grip his heart. He had felt the horrid fear of defeat striking at his soul. Upon him were the marks of the conflict. His victory had not been won without effort. Success had demanded a price and he had paid. Perhaps no one but the man himself knew how great was the price he had paid.

The man found also that Success brought cares greater than he had ever known in the days of his struggle. Always there are cares that wait at the end of the battle and attend only upon the victor. Always there are responsibilities that come only when the victory is won--that are never seen in the heat of the conflict.

Once let it be discovered that you have the strength and the willingness to carry burdens and burdens will be heaped upon you until you stagger, fainting, under the load. Life has never yet bred a man who could shoulder the weight that the world insists that he take up in his success. And, when the man could not carry all the burdens that the world brought because his strength and endurance was only that of a mortal, the world cursed him--called him selfish, full of greed, heartless, an oppressor caring nothing for the woes of others. Those who had offered no helping hand in the time of his need now clamored loudly for a large part of his strength. Those who had cared nothing for his life in the times of his hardships now insisted that he give the larger part of his life to them. Those who had held him back now demanded that he lift them up to a place beside him. Those who had shown him only indifference--coldness--contempt, now begged of him attention--friendship--honors--aid.

And from all these things that attended his success the man found it impossible to escape. The cares, the burdens, the responsibilities that Success forced him to take up rested heavily upon him. So heavy indeed were these things that he had little strength or will left for the enjoyment of that which he had so worthily won.

And the victory that he had so hardily gained, the place that he now held, the man found that he could keep only by the utmost exertion of his strength. The battles he had fought were nothing in comparison to those he must now fight. The struggle he had made was nothing to the effort he must continue to make. Temptations multiplied and appeared in many new and unexpected forms. The very world that pointed him out as an example watched eagerly for excuse to condemn. Those who sought him with honors--who praised and flattered him, in envy, secretly hoped for his ruin. Those who followed him like dogs for favors would howl like wolves on his trail if he turned ever so little aside. Those who opened for him the doors of opportunities would flock like vultures to carrion if he should fall. The world, that, without consideration, heaped upon him its burdens, would trample him beneath its feet if he should slip under the weight. Nor had he in Success won freedom. His very servants were freer than he, to come and go, to seek their peculiar pleasures.

The chains with which Success had fettered the man were unusually galling and heavy upon him that day, when, on his way to an important appointment, his carriage was checked in a crowded street. The man's mind was so absorbed in the business waiting his attention that he did not notice how dense was the crowd that barred the way. Impatiently--with overwrought nerves--he spoke sharply, commanding his man to drive on.

The man begged pardon but it was impossible.

"Impossible," still more sharply, "what's the matter?"

The driver ventured a smile, "It's the circus parade, sir."

"Then turn around."

But that, too, was impossible. The traffic had pushed in behind hemming them in.

Then, down the street that crossed in front of the crowded jam of vehicles, came the familiar sound of trumpets and the gorgeously attired heralds at the head of the procession appeared, followed by the leading band with its crashing, smashing, music.

As gilded chariot followed gilded chariot, each drawn by many pairs of beautiful horses, gaily plumed and equipped--as the many riders, in glittering armor and flashing, spangled, costumes, rode proudly past; followed by the long line of elephants and camels with the cages of their fellow captives; and, in turn, by the chariot racers, the clowns, and the wagons of black faced fun makers; and at last by the steam calliope with its escort of madly shouting urchins--the man in the carriage slipped away from the cares and burdens of the present into the freedom of his Yesterdays. He escaped from the galling chains that Success had put upon him and lived again a circus day in the long ago.

Weeks before the date of the great event, the barns and sheds and every available wall in the little village, to which the boy often went with his father, would be covered with gorgeous pictures announcing the many startling, stupendous, wonders, to be seen for so small a price. There was a hippopotamus of such size that a boat load of twenty naked savages was not for him a mouthful. There were elephants so huge that the house where the boy lived was but a play house beside them. There were troops of aerial artists, who, on wires and rings and trapeze and ladders and ropes, did daring, dreadful, death defying, deeds, that no simian in his old world forest would ever think of attempting. There was a great, glittering, gorgeous, procession, of such length that the farther end was lost beyond the distant horizon and tents that covered more acres of ground than the boy could see from the top of the orchard hill.

Wonderful promises of the billboards! Wonderful! Wonderful promises of the billboards of Life! Wonderful!

Then would follow the days of waiting--the endless days of waiting--when the boy, with the help of the little girl, would try to be everything that the billboards pictured, from the roaring lion in his cage to the painted clown who cut such side splitting capers and the human fly that, with her gay Japanese parasol, walked upside down upon a polished ceiling. When circus day was coming, the fairies and knights and princes and soldiers and all their tried and true companions were forced to go somewhere--anywhere--out of the boy's way. There was no time, in those busy days, even for fishing. The old mill pond had no charm that was not exceeded by the promises of the billboards. The earth itself, indeed, was merely a place upon which to pitch a circus tent. The charms of the little girl, even, were almost totally eclipsed by the captivating loveliness of those ladies who, in spangled tights of blue and pink and red, hung by their teeth at dizzy heights, bestrode glittering wheels upon slack wires, or were shot from cannon to soar, amid black smoke and lurid flame, like angels, far above the heads of the common people.

There was no lying in bed to be called the third time the morning of that day; when at last it came. Scarcely had the sun peeped through the orchard on the hill when the boy was up and at the window anxiously looking to see if the sky was clear. Very early the start for town was made for there is much on circus day that is not pictured on the billboards--*that*, of course, the boy knew. And, as they drove through the fresh smelling fields, the boy would wonder if the long journey would ever come to an end and would ask himself, with sinking heart: "What if they had mistaken the day? What if something had happened that the circus could not materialize the promises of the billboards? What, if the hippopotamus, the elephants, the beautiful ladies in spangles and tights, and all the other promises of the billboards should fail?" And somewhere, deep within his being, the boy would feel a thrill of gladness that the little girl was so close beside him. If anything should happen that the promises of the billboards should fail he would need the little girl. While, if nothing happened--if it was all as pictured--still it would not be enough if the little girl were not there.

It was all over at last. The spangled riders galloped out of the ring; the trapeze performers made their last death defying leap; the clown cracked his last joke and cut his last caper; the last peanut in the sack was devoured by the elephant; and, at the close of the long day, the boy and the girl went back through the quiet fields to their homes; tired with the excitement and wonder of it all but with sighs of content and happiness. And, deep in his heart, that night, the boy resolved that he would grow up to travel with a circus. He would be very sorry to leave father and mother and the little girl but nothing in the world--nothing--should keep him from such a glorious career.

The man knew, now, that the promises of those billboards in his Yesterdays were never fulfilled. He knew, now, that the golden chariots were not gold at all but only gilded. He knew, now, that those wondrous beings who wore the glittering, spangled, costumes, were only very common and very ordinary men and women. He did not, now, envy the riders in the procession or the performers in the tent. He knew that to have a place in the parade or to perform in the ring, is to envy those whose applause you must win. The quiet of the old fields; the peaceful home under the orchard hill; the gentle companionship of the little girl; these were the things that in the man's life endured long after the glamor of the circus was gone.

Through the circus day crowd the man was driven on to his appointment but his mind was not now occupied with the business that awaited him. His thoughts were not with the crowd that filled the streets. His heart was in his Yesterdays. The music of the circus band, the sight of the parade that so stirred his memories of childhood, had awakened within him a hunger for the old home scenes. He longed to escape from Success--to get away from the circus parade of Life in which he found himself riding. He was weary of performing in the ring. He wanted to go home through the quiet fields. Perhaps--perhaps--amid the scenes of his Yesterdays, he might find that which Success had not brought.

As quickly as he could make arrangements, he went.

Of the woman's success, I cannot write here. My story has been poorly told, indeed, if I have not made it clear that, for this woman who knew herself to be a woman, Success was inseparable from Love.

For every woman who knows herself to be a woman, Love and Success are one.

LOVE

AGAIN it was that time of the year when every corner of the world is a lovers' corner.

On bough and branch, in orchard and wood; on bush and vine, in garden and yard; in meadow grass and pasture sod; on the silvery lichens that cling to the rocks; among the ferns and mosses that dwell in cool retreats; amid the reeds and rushes by the old mill pond; in the fragrant mints and fluted blades on the banks of the little creek; the children of Nature sought their mates or by their mates were sought.

Every flower cup was a loving cup, lifted to drink a pledge to Life; every tint of color was a blush of love, called forth by the wooing of Life; every perfumed breath was a breath of love, a blessing and prayer of Life; every rustling movement was a whisper of love, a promised word of Life; every touch of the breeze was a caress of love, a passionate kiss of Life; every sunbeam was a smile of love, warm with the tender triumph of Life.

The bees, that, in their labor for hive and swarm, carry the golden pollen from flower to flower, preach thus the word of God. The gauze winged insects, that, in the evening, dance their aerial mating dance, declare thus the Creator's will. The fireflies, that, in the night time, light their tiny lamps of love, signal thus a message from the throne on high.

The fowls of the air, singing their mating songs; the wild stallion on the hills, trumpeting aloud his fiery strength; the bull on the plains, thundering his bellowing challenge; the panther that in the mountains screams to his mate; the wolf that in the timber howls to his mistress; declare thus the supreme law of Life--make known the unchanging purpose of God--and evidence an authority and power divine.

In all this wooing and mating; in all this seeking and being sought; in all this giving and receiving; in all this loving and being loved; in all natural and holy desire; Life is exalted--the divine is worshiped--acceptable offerings to God are made.

To preserve Life--to perpetuate Life--to produce Life--to perfect Life--to exalt Life--this is the purpose of Life. In all the activity of Life there is no other meaning manifest. This, indeed, *is* Life. How foolish then to think only of eternal Life as though it began at the grave. This Life that *is*, is the eternal Life. Eternity is to-day. The man and woman who mate in love fulfill thus the eternal law of Life, and, in their children, conceived and born in Love, do they know and do the will of God, even as do all things that are alive.

Life and Love are one.

The man had been at his boyhood home but three days when the neighbor, who lived next door, told him that his childhood playmate was coming, with her aunt, to visit their old home for a few weeks.

"Needs a rest and quiet" the neighbor said; and smiled at nothing at all as neighbors will sometimes do.

Perhaps, though, the neighbor smiled at the look of surprise and bewilderment that swept over the man's face as he heard the news, or it might have been at the mingling of pleasure and regret that was in his voice as he answered: "Indeed." Or, perhaps, the neighbor was wondering what the woman would say and how she would look if she knew that the man was to be next door. Whatever the reason the neighbor smiled.

They did not know that the woman was, in reality, seeking to escape from the thought of Failure that so haunted her. Since that day when her good friend had talked to her of her career and had gravely asked--"for *you* do you think it would be success?"--her work had become more and more unbearable. In desperation, at last, she had arranged to go, for a few weeks, back to the scenes of her girlhood; hoping to find there, as she had found before, the peace and strength she needed.

The cherry tree, in the corner of the garden near the hedge, showered the delicate petals of its blossoms down with every touch of the gentle breeze. In the nearby bower of green, a pair of brown birds had just put the finishing touch to a new nest. But, in the years that had passed since that boy and girl play wedding, the tree had grown large, and scarred, and old. Many pairs of brown birds had nested and reared their broods in the hedge since that day when the lad had kissed his childhood mate with a kiss that was different. And the little opening through which the boy and girl had so often gone at each other's call was closed by a growth of branches that time had woven as if to shut, forever, that gateway of their Yesterdays. On his former visit, the man had looked for that gateway of his childhood but could not find it. And now, when he heard that she was coming, he went again, curiously, to see if he could find any sign to show where the opening had been. But the branches that the years had woven hid from the man's eyes every trace of the old way that, in his Yesterdays, had been so plain.

Late that afternoon, when the neighbor, coming from the depot with his guests, drove slowly up the hill, the man stood at the gate where, years before, the little boy had sat on the post, and, swinging his bare legs, had watched the big wagons, loaded with household goods, turning into the yard of the place next door.

There was no reason why the man should get up when the first touches of gray light showed in the eastern sky the next morning, but the day seemed to call him and he arose and went out. From the little hill where he had sat that day when first he knew that he was a man and where his manhood life began with his dreams, he watched the sun rise and saw the sleeping world awake. Then back through the orchard that was all dew drenched and ringing with the morning hymn of the birds, he went, until he stood in the garden.

The man did not know why he went into the garden. Something seemed to lead him there. And he went very softly as one goes into places that are holy with the memories of dead years. Very still, he stood, watching the two birds that had built their nest in the hedge near the cherry tree that, now, lifted its branches so high. The two birds were very, very, busy that morning; but, busy as they were, the father bird could not resist pouring forth the joy of his life in a flood of melody while his mate, swinging and fluttering and chirping on a nearby twig, seemed to enter as fully and heartily into his sentiments as though the song were her own. Breathlessly, with bare head and upturned, eager, face, the man watched and listened.

When the song was ended he drew a long breath--then started and, without moving from his place, looked carefully around. A low call had reached his ears--a familiar call that seemed to come out of the long ago. Surely his fancy was playing him strange tricks that morning.

He was turning toward the house when, again, that call came--low and clear. It was a call of his Yesterdays. And this time it was followed by a low, full throated laugh that was as full of music as the song of the bird to which the man had been listening.

With amazement and wonder upon his face, he turned quickly toward the hedge, as a voice that was like an echo of the laugh said: "Good morning! Pardon me for startling you--you looked so much like the little boy that I couldn't resist."

"But where are you?" asked the man, bewildered still.

Again came that low, full throated laugh. Then: "I believe you think I am a ghost. I'm here at the hedge--at the old place. Have you forgotten?"

Slowly, as she spoke, he went toward the hedge, guided by her voice. "So *you* found it then," he said slowly, gazing at the beautiful woman face that was framed in the green of the leaves and branches.

And at his words, the woman's heart beat quicker--so he had *tried* to find it--but aloud she only said: "Of course."

To which he returned smilingly: "But it is quite grown over now, isn't it? You could scarcely come through there now as you used to do--could you?"

The woman laughed again. "I could if I were a man"--she challenged.

A moment later he stood beside her; a little breathless, with his clothing disarranged, and a scratch or two on his face and hands.

"Do you know"--she said when they had shaken hands quite properly as grown up people must do--"do you know that I was dreadfully afraid to meet you? When they told me that you were here I wanted to go away again. I was afraid that you would be so different. Do you understand?"

"Yes," he said, gravely, "I understand." But he did not tell her, then, how fully he understood.

She went on: "But when I looked through the hedge and saw you with your hat off, watching the birds, I knew you were the same little boy--and--well--I could not resist giving the old call."

And, all at once, the man knew why he had risen early that morning and why he had gone into the garden.

After that, they spent many days together in the scenes of their childhood; living over again, so far as man and woman may, their Yesterdays. And so cane, at last, the day that was forever after, to them, *the* day of all their days.

It was in the afternoon and they were together down by the little brook, in the shade of the willows, where the stream, running lazily under the patches of light and shade, murmured drowsily--seeming more than half asleep. She was weaving an old time daisy chain from a great armful that he had helped her gather on their way to the cool retreat. A bit of fancy work that she had brought from the house lay neglected near his hat, which the man, boy like, had cast aside. He was industriously fishing for minnows, with a slender twig of willow for a rod, a line of thread from her sewing, and a pin, that she had found for him, fashioned into a hook. With a pointed stick he had dug among the roots of the old tree for bait--securing one, tiny, thin, worm and rejoicing gleefully at his success. For a long time neither had said a word; but the woman, her white fingers busy with the daisies in her lap, had several times looked up from her pretty task to smile at the man who was so intensely and seriously interested in his childish sport.

"Gee! I nearly got one that time!" He exclaimed with boyish triumph and disappointment in his voice.

The woman laughed merrily. "One would think," she said, "that your fame in life depended upon your catching one of those poor little fish. What do you suppose your dear, devoted, public would say if they could see you now?"

The man grunted his disapproval. "I came out here to get away from said public," he retorted. "Why do you drag 'em into our paradise?"

At his words, a warm color crept into the woman's face, and, bending low over the daisies in her lap, she did not answer.

Lifting the improvised fishing tackle of his childhood and looking at it critically the man said: "I suppose, now, that if this rod were a split bamboo, and this thread were braided silk, and this pin with its wiggly piece of worm were a "Silver Doctor" or a "Queen of the Waters" or a "Dusty Miller" or a "Brown Hackle"; and if this stream were an educated stream, with educated trout; and the house up there were a club house; and your dear old aunt, who is watching to see that I don't eat you, were a lot of whist playing old men; I suppose you would think it all right and a proper sport for a man. But for me--I can't see much difference--except that, just now--" he carefully lowered his hook into the water--"just now, I prefer this. In fact," he added meditatively, "I would rather do this than anything else in the world."

The color in the woman's face deepened.

After a little, he looked cautiously around to see her bending over the daisy chain. A moment later, under pretense of examining his bait, he stole another look. Then, in spite of his declaration, he abandoned his sport to stretch himself full length on the ground at her side.

She did not look at him but bent her head low over the wealth of white and gold blossoms in her lap; and the man noticed, with an odd feeling of pleasure, the beautiful curve of her white neck from the soft brown hair to the edge of her dress low on the shoulder. Then, with a sly smile, as the boy of their Yesterdays might have done, he stealthily raised the slender willow twig and with the tip cautiously attempted to lift the thin golden chain that she always wore loosely about her throat with the locket or pendant concealed by her dress.

She clutched the chain with a frightened gesture and a little exclamation. "You must not--you must not do that."

The man laughed aloud as the mischievous boy would have laughed.

But the woman, with flaming cheeks, caught the twig from his hand and threw it into the creek. "If you are not good, I shall call auntie," she threatened.

At which he looked ruefully toward the porch and became very serious. "Do you know that I am going away to-morrow?" he asked.

"And leave your paradise for your dear public?" she said mockingly. "The public will be glad."

"And you, will you care?"

"I'm going back to my work, too, next week," she replied.

"But will you care to-morrow?" he persisted.

The woman's fingers, busy with the daisy chain, trembled.

The man, when she still did not answer his question, arose and, picking up his hat and her sewing, held out his hand.

She looked up into his face questioningly.

"Come"--he said with a grave smile--"come."

Still without speaking, she gave him her hand and he helped her to her feet; and, at her touch, the man again felt that thrill of pleasure.

The aunt, from her place on the porch, saw them coming up the grassy slope, through the daisies, toward the house. She saw them coming and smiled--as the neighbor had smiled, so she smiled, apparently, at nothing at all.

But the man and the woman did not go to the porch where the old lady sat. With a wave of their hands, they passed from her sight around the house, and, a few minutes later, stood face to face in that quiet, secluded, corner of the garden, under the old cherry tree, close by the hedge.

"Now," said the man gently, "now tell me--will you be sorry to have me go away to-morrow?"

She made no pretense that she did not understand, Nor did she hesitate as one in doubt. Lifting her head, proudly, humbly, graciously, she looked at him and, in that look, surrendered to him, without reserve, all the treasures of her womanhood that, with such care, she had kept against that hour. And her face was shining with the light that only a woman's mate can kindle.

The man caught his breath. "My wife," he said. "My wife,"

A few moments later he whispered: "Tell me again--I know that you have always belonged to me and I to you--but tell me again--you will--you will--be my wife?"

Releasing herself gently, she lifted her hands and, unfastening that slender chain of gold from around her throat, with rosy cheeks and happy, tender, eyes, held out to him a tiny brass ring.

So the Yesterdays of the man and the Yesterdays of the woman became Their Yesterdays.

All that Dreams, Occupation, Knowledge, Ignorance, Religion, Tradition, Temptation, Life, Death, Failure, Success, Love and Memories had given him, this man who knew that he was a man, gave to her. All that the Thirteen Truly Great Things of Life had given her, this woman who knew herself to be a woman, gave to him. And thus these two became one. As God made them one, they became one.

And this is the love that I say, is one of the Thirteen Truly Great Things of Life.

But my story is not yet quite finished for still, you must know, there are Memories.

MEMORIES

AND the years of the man and the woman passed until all their days were Yesterdays.

Even as they had, together, crossed the threshold of the old, old, door that has stood open since the beginning, they stood now, together, upon the threshold of another door that has never been closed.

And it was so, that, as once they went back into the Yesterdays that became Their Yesterdays, so they still went back to the days that were past. It was so, that the things of their manhood and womanhood had become to them, now, even as the things of their childhood. They knew, now, that, indeed, the work of men is but the play of children, after all.

Their years were nearly spent, it is true. His hair was silvery white and his form was bent and trembling. Her cheeks were like the drying petals of a rose and her once brown hair was as white as his. But the vigor and strength and life of their years lived still--gloriously increased in the lives that they had given to the race.

Gone were the years of their manhood and womanhood--even as the days of their boyhood and girlhood--they were gone. But, as the boy and the girl had lived in the man and the woman, the man and the woman lived, now, in their boys and girls and in the children of their children.

And this was the true glory and the fulfillment of their lives--that they could live thus in their children--that they could see themselves renewed in their children and in their children's children.

So it was that Memories became to this man and this woman, also, one of the Thirteen Truly Great Things of Life.

There are many things that might be told about this man and woman--about the work they did, the place they held in life, and the rewards and honors they received--but I have put down all that, at the end, seemed of any importance to them. Therefore have I put down all that matters to my story.

What matters to them and to my story is this: always, as they went back into the Yesterdays, they went back to the days of their childhood and to the days of their children. They went back only to *Their* Yesterdays. To those other days--those days when they were strangers--they did not go back.

THE END.

www.bookjungle.com *email:* sales@bookjungle.com *fax:* 630-214-0564 *mail:* Book Jungle PO Box 2226 Champaign, IL 61825

The Codes Of Hammurabi And Moses
W. W. Davies

QTY

The discovery of the Hammurabi Code is one of the greatest achievements of archaeology, and is of paramount interest, not only to the student of the Bible, but also to all those interested in ancient history...

Religion   ISBN: *1-59462-338-4*   Pages:132
MSRP $12.95

The Theory of Moral Sentiments
Adam Smith

QTY

This work from 1749. contains original theories of conscience amd moral judgment and it is the foundation for systemof morals.

Philosophy   ISBN: *1-59462-777-0*   Pages:536
MSRP $19.95

Jessica's First Prayer
Hesba Stretton

QTY

In a screened and secluded corner of one of the many railway-bridges which span the streets of London there could be seen a few years ago, from five o'clock every morning until half past eight, a tidily set-out coffee-stall, consisting of a trestle and board, upon which stood two large tin cans, with a small fire of charcoal burning under each so as to keep the coffee boiling during the early hours of the morning when the work-people were thronging into the city on their way to their daily toil...

Childrens   ISBN: *1-59462-373-2*   Pages:84
MSRP $9.95

My Life and Work
Henry Ford

QTY

Henry Ford revolutionized the world with his implementation of mass production for the Model T automobile. Gain valuable business insight into his life and work with his own auto-biography... "We have only started on our development of our country we have not as yet, with all our talk of wonderful progress, done more than scratch the surface. The progress has been wonderful enough but..."

Biographies/   ISBN: *1-59462-198-5*   Pages:300
MSRP $21.95

www.bookjungle.com *email: sales@bookjungle.com fax: 630-214-0564 mail: Book Jungle PO Box 2226 Champaign, IL 61825*

The Art of Cross-Examination
Francis Wellman

I presume it is the experience of every author, after his first book is published upon an important subject, to be almost overwhelmed with a wealth of ideas and illustrations which could readily have been included in his book, and which to his own mind, at least, seem to make a second edition inevitable. Such certainly was the case with me; and when the first edition had reached its sixth impression in five months, I rejoiced to learn that it seemed to my publishers that the book had met with a sufficiently favorable reception to justify a second and considerably enlarged edition. ..

QTY

Reference   ISBN: *1-59462-647-2*   Pages:412 MSRP $19.95

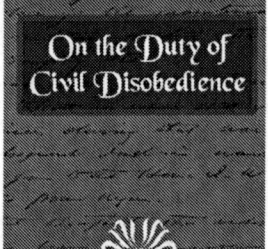

On the Duty of Civil Disobedience
Henry David Thoreau

Thoreau wrote his famous essay, On the Duty of Civil Disobedience, as a protest against an unjust but popular war and the immoral but popular institution of slave-owning. He did more than write—he declined to pay his taxes, and was hauled off to gaol in consequence. Who can say how much this refusal of his hastened the end of the war and of slavery ?

QTY

Law   ISBN: *1-59462-747-9*   Pages:48 MSRP $7.45

Dream Psychology Psychoanalysis for Beginners
Sigmund Freud

Sigmund Freud, born Sigismund Schlomo Freud (May 6, 1856 - September 23, 1939), was a Jewish-Austrian neurologist and psychiatrist who co-founded the psychoanalytic school of psychology. Freud is best known for his theories of the unconscious mind, especially involving the mechanism of repression; his redefinition of sexual desire as mobile and directed towards a wide variety of objects; and his therapeutic techniques, especially his understanding of transference in the therapeutic relationship and the presumed value of dreams as sources of insight into unconscious desires.

QTY

Psychology   ISBN: *1-59462-905-6*   Pages:196 MSRP $15.45

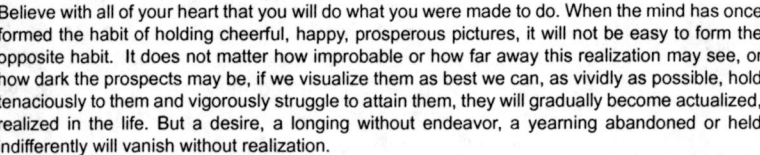

The Miracle of Right Thought
Orison Swett Marden

Believe with all of your heart that you will do what you were made to do. When the mind has once formed the habit of holding cheerful, happy, prosperous pictures, it will not be easy to form the opposite habit. It does not matter how improbable or how far away this realization may see, or how dark the prospects may be, if we visualize them as best we can, as vividly as possible, hold tenaciously to them and vigorously struggle to attain them, they will gradually become actualized, realized in the life. But a desire, a longing without endeavor, a yearning abandoned or held indifferently will vanish without realization.

QTY

Self Help   ISBN: *1-59462-644-8*   Pages:360 MSRP $25.45

www.bookjungle.com *email: sales@bookjungle.com fax: 630-214-0564 mail: Book Jungle PO Box 2226 Champaign, IL 61825*

QTY

☐ **The Rosicrucian Cosmo-Conception Mystic Christianity** *by Max Heindel*   ISBN: *1-59462-188-8*   **$38.95**
The Rosicrucian Cosmo-conception is not dogmatic, neither does it appeal to any other authority than the reason of the student. It is; not controversial, but is; sent forth in the, hope that it may help to clear..   New Age/Religion Pages 646

☐ **Abandonment To Divine Providence** *by Jean-Pierre de Caussade*   ISBN: *1-59462-228-0*   **$25.95**
"The Rev. Jean Pierre de Caussade was one of the most remarkable spiritual writers of the Society of Jesus in France in the 18th Century. His death took place at Toulouse in 1751. His works have gone through many editions and have been republished...   Inspirational/Religion Pages 400

☐ **Mental Chemistry** *by Charles Haanel*   ISBN: *1-59462-192-6*   **$23.95**
Mental Chemistry allows the change of material conditions by combining and appropriately utilizing the power of the mind. Much like applied chemistry creates something new and unique out of careful combinations of chemicals the mastery of mental chemistry...   New Age Pages 354

☐ **The Letters of Robert Browning and Elizabeth Barret Barrett 1845-1846 vol II**   ISBN: *1-59462-193-4*   **$35.95**
by Robert Browning and Elizabeth Barrett   Biographies Pages 596

☐ **Gleanings In Genesis (volume I)** *by Arthur W. Pink*   ISBN: *1-59462-130-6*   **$27.45**
Appropriately has Genesis been termed "the seed plot of the Bible" for in it we have, in germ form, almost all of the great doctrines which are afterwards fully developed in the books of Scripture which follow...   Religion/Inspirational Pages 420

☐ **The Master Key** *by L. W. de Laurence*   ISBN: *1-59462-001-6*   **$30.95**
In no branch of human knowledge has there been a more lively increase of the spirit of research during the past few years than in the study of Psychology, Concentration and Mental Discipline. The requests for authentic lessons in Thought Control, Mental Discipline and...   New Age/Business Pages 422

☐ **The Lesser Key Of Solomon Goetia** *by L. W. de Laurence*   ISBN: *1-59462-092-X*   **$9.95**
This translation of the first book of the "Lernegton" which is here for the first time made accessible to students of Talismanic Magic was done, after careful collation and edition, from numerous Ancient Manuscripts in Hebrew, Latin, and French...   New Age/Occult Pages 92

☐ **Rubaiyat Of Omar Khayyam** *by Edward Fitzgerald*   ISBN: *1-59462-332-5*   **$13.95**
Edward Fitzgerald, whom the world has already learned, in spite of his own efforts to remain within the shadow of anonymity, to look upon as one of the rarest poets of the century, was born at Bredfield, in Suffolk, on the 31st of March, 1809. He was the third son of John Purcell...   Music Pages 172

☐ **Ancient Law** *by Henry Maine*   ISBN: *1-59462-128-4*   **$29.95**
The chief object of the following pages is to indicate some of the earliest ideas of mankind, as they are reflected in Ancient Law, and to point out the relation of those ideas to modern thought.   Religion/History Pages 452

☐ **Far-Away Stories** *by William J. Locke*   ISBN: *1-59462-129-2*   **$19.45**
"Good wine needs no bush, but a collection of mixed vintages does. And this book is just such a collection. Some of the stories I do not want to remain buried for ever in the museum files of dead magazine-numbers an author's not unpardonable vanity..."   Fiction Pages 272

☐ **Life of David Crockett** *by David Crockett*   ISBN: *1-59462-250-7*   **$27.45**
"Colonel David Crockett was one of the most remarkable men of the times in which he lived. Born in humble life, but gifted with a strong will, an indomitable courage, and unremitting perseverance..   Biographies/New Age Pages 424

☐ **Lip-Reading** *by Edward Nitchie*   ISBN: *1-59462-206-X*   **$25.95**
Edward B. Nitchie, founder of the New York School for the Hard of Hearing, now the Nitchie School of Lip-Reading, Inc, wrote "LIP-READING Principles and Practice". The development and perfecting of this meritorious work on lip-reading was an undertaking...   How-to Pages 400

☐ **A Handbook of Suggestive Therapeutics, Applied Hypnotism, Psychic Science**   ISBN: *1-59462-214-0*   **$24.95**
by Henry Munro   Health/New Age/Health/Self-help Pages 376

☐ **A Doll's House: and Two Other Plays** *by Henrik Ibsen*   ISBN: *1-59462-112-8*   **$19.95**
Henrik Ibsen created this classic when in revolutionary 1848 Rome. Introducing some striking concepts in playwriting for the realist genre, this play has been studied the world over.   Fiction/Classics/Plays 308

☐ **The Light of Asia** *by sir Edwin Arnold*   ISBN: *1-59462-204-3*   **$13.95**
In this poetic masterpiece, Edwin Arnold describes the life and teachings of Buddha. The man who was to become known as Buddha to the world was born as Prince Gautama of India but he rejected the worldly riches and abandoned the reigns of power when...   Religion/History/Biographies Pages 170

☐ **The Complete Works of Guy de Maupassant** *by Guy de Maupassant*   ISBN: *1-59462-157-8*   **$16.95**
"For days and days, nights and nights, I had dreamed of that first kiss which was to consecrate our engagement, and I knew not on what spot I should put my lips..."   Fiction/Classics Pages 240

☐ **The Art of Cross-Examination** *by Francis L. Wellman*   ISBN: *1-59462-309-0*   **$26.95**
Written by a renowned trial lawyer, Wellman imparts his experience and uses case studies to explain how to use psychology to extract desired information through questioning.   How-to/Science/Reference Pages 408

☐ **Answered or Unanswered?** *by Louisa Vaughan*   ISBN: *1-59462-248-5*   **$10.95**
Miracles of Faith in China   Religion Pages 112

☐ **The Edinburgh Lectures on Mental Science (1909)** *by Thomas*   ISBN: *1-59462-008-3*   **$11.95**
This book contains the substance of a course of lectures recently given by the writer in the Queen Street Hall, Edinburgh. Its purpose is to indicate the Natural Principles governing the relation between Mental Action and Material Conditions...   New Age/Psychology Pages 148

☐ **Ayesha** *by H. Rider Haggard*   ISBN: *1-59462-301-5*   **$24.95**
Verily and indeed it is the unexpected that happens! Probably if there was one person upon the earth from whom the Editor of this, and of a certain previous history, did not expect to hear again...   Classics Pages 380

☐ **Ayala's Angel** *by Anthony Trollope*   ISBN: *1-59462-352-X*   **$29.95**
The two girls were both pretty; but Lucy who was twenty-one who supposed to be simple and comparatively unattractive, whereas Ayala was credited, as her Bombwhat romantic name might show, with poetic charm and a taste for romance. Ayala when her father died was nineteen...   Fiction Pages 484

☐ **The American Commonwealth** *by James Bryce*   ISBN: *1-59462-286-8*   **$34.45**
An interpretation of American democratic political theory. It examines political mechanics and society from the perspective of Scotsman James Bryce   Politics Pages 572

☐ **Stories of the Pilgrims** *by Margaret P. Pumphrey*   ISBN: *1-59462-116-0*   **$17.95**
This book explores pilgrims religious oppression in England as well as their escape to Holland and eventual crossing to America on the Mayflower, and their early days in New England.   History Pages 268

www.bookjungle.com email: sales@bookjungle.com fax: 630-214-0564 mail: Book Jungle PO Box 2226 Champaign, IL 61825

QTY

The Fasting Cure by *Sinclair Upton* ISBN: *1-59462-222-1* **$13.95**
In the Cosmopolitan Magazine for May, 1910, and in the Contemporary Review (London) for April, 1910, I published an article dealing with my experiences in fasting. I have written a great many magazine articles, but never one which attracted so much attention... New Age/Self Help/Health Pages 164

Hebrew Astrology by *Sepharial* ISBN: *1-59462-308-2* **$13.45**
In these days of advanced thinking it is a matter of common observation that we have left many of the old landmarks behind and that we are now pressing forward to greater heights and to a wider horizon than that which represented the mind-content of our progenitors... Astrology Pages 144

Thought Vibration or The Law of Attraction in the Thought World ISBN: *1-59462-127-6* **$12.95**
by *William Walker Atkinson* Psychology/Religion Pages 144

Optimism by *Helen Keller* ISBN: *1-59462-108-X* **$15.95**
Helen Keller was blind, deaf, and mute since 19 months old, yet famously learned how to overcome these handicaps, communicate with the world, and spread her lectures promoting optimism. An inspiring read for everyone... Biographies/Inspirational Pages 84

Sara Crewe by *Frances Burnett* ISBN: *1-59462-360-0* **$9.45**
In the first place, Miss Minchin lived in London. Her home was a large, dull, tall one, in a large, dull square, where all the houses were alike, and all the sparrows were alike, and where all the door-knockers made the same heavy sound... Childrens/Classic Pages 88

The Autobiography of Benjamin Franklin by *Benjamin Franklin* ISBN: *1-59462-135-7* **$24.95**
The Autobiography of Benjamin Franklin has probably been more extensively read than any other American historical work, and no other book of its kind has had such ups and downs of fortune. Franklin lived for many years in England, where he was agent... Biographies/History Pages 332

Name	
Email	
Telephone	
Address	
City, State ZIP	

☐ Credit Card   ☐ Check / Money Order

Credit Card Number	
Expiration Date	
Signature	

Please Mail to: Book Jungle
PO Box 2226
Champaign, IL 61825
or Fax to: 630-214-0564

ORDERING INFORMATION
web: www.bookjungle.com
email: sales@bookjungle.com
fax: 630-214-0564
mail: Book Jungle PO Box 2226 Champaign, IL 61825
or PayPal to sales@bookjungle.com

Please contact us for bulk discounts

DIRECT-ORDER TERMS

**20% Discount if You Order
Two or More Books**
Free Domestic Shipping!
Accepted: Master Card, Visa,
Discover, American Express

Printed in the United States
91416LV00005B/35/A